DATE DUE

JUN 2 2 2001	
OCT 0 4 2001	
NOV 0 3 2001	
NOV 2 7 2001	
MAY 1 6 2002	
SEP 1 5 2002	
APR 1 8 2004	
FEB 0 5 2006	

The Ghost
of
Honeymoon Creek

by

Raymond Bial

with illustrations by
Anna Bial

Face to Face Books
Shorewood, Wisconsin

Face to Face Books is an imprint of Midwest Traditions, Inc.,
a nonprofit organization working to help preserve a sense of place
and tradition in American life.

For a catalog of books, write:
Face to Face Books / Midwest Traditions
3710 N. Morris Blvd.
Shorewood, Wisconsin 53211
U.S.A.
or call 1-800-736-9189

Library of Congress Cataloging-in-Publication Data

Bial, Raymond.
　　　　The ghost of Honeymoon Creek / by Raymond Bial ; with illustrations
by Anna Bial. — 1st ed.
　　　　　　　p.　　　cm.
　　　　Sequel to: The fresh grave.
　　　　Summary: Hank and his 'fraidy-cat buddy Clifford are chased by a host
of ghosts through the countryside near Myrtleville and encounter a mysterious
old lady who leads them to discover the secret of the ghost of Honeymoon Creek.
　　　　　　　ISBN 1-883953-28-6 (hc. : alk. paper). — ISBN 1-883953-27-8 (pbk.
: alk. paper)
　　　　　　　[1. Ghosts Fiction.]　　I. Bial, Anna, ill.　　II. Title.
PZ7.B46995Gh　1999
[Fic] — dc21

　　　　　　　　　　　　　　　　　　　99-40590
　　　　　　　　　　　　　　　　　　　CIP

First Edition
10 9 8 7 6 5 4 3 2 1

for Sarah

Chapter I

Hank knew they shouldn't go back there. Just thinking of the old Hawkins Farm tended to snatch the breath right out of him. For years, on moonlit nights, folks had claimed they'd seen a misty white figure hovering over Honeymoon Creek not far from the old homestead. It could have been Old Man Crupp's bull, Lucifer. Or mist floating over the water. Then again, in his heart, Hank knew it was a restless spirit — because he had seen her face.

As usual, it was Clifford who brought it up. "I hear a light goes on every night in the window of that old spook house!" he said to Mary Ethel Freeny, Rosie Morgan, and a few other kids gathered around the liars' bench in front of Tremont's Drugstore and Fountain.

"You mean there *really* is somebody in that old house?" asked Mary Ethel, her auburn eyes magnified behind the thick lenses of her glasses. "I knew that Honeymoon Creek is haunted. But there's never been a ghost inhabiting that house!"

"Could be the same ghost that's haunted the creek all these years!" Clifford declared. A foot shorter than most everybody else in the world, Clifford tried to compensate for his lack of height by the sheer output of his mouth. Then again, his mouth was fueled by great excesses of his imagination, often propelling Hank and Clifford on risky adventures. For this reason, Hank was more than a little cautious about getting mixed up in yet another of Clifford's schemes, especially if it involved setting so much as one foot on Old Man Crupp's land.

Wide-eyed, Mary Ethel gazed adoringly at Clifford. A girl with spirally red hair and abundant freckles, she said, "I wonder who — or what — could be back in that house."

"Could be criminals. Maybe even murderers," Clifford pronounced with an air of authority. "Yep, that's it. Criminals who don't know about the ghost of Honeymoon Creek. Or it could be another ghost that doesn't know the place is already haunted — or is trying to chase out the original ghost!"

Hank snorted. "Could be nobody."

Clifford swelled up like a bullfrog. "Well, if there's nobody back there, how come you don't want to go?"

"'Cause I've got too much sense," Hank said right back at him. He and Clifford were complete opposites, which probably explained why they had always been best friends. "What if the ghost caught us?"

Briefly, the two young men glared at each other. Hank never liked to take unneccesary risks, but if caught up in a dangerous situation, he never hesitated to stand up for himself — and for others. In contrast, Clifford was as reckless as he was cowardly, which Hank knew from experience was a volatile combination. A sturdy farm boy, blond and blue-eyed, Hank valued honest labor. Whereas Clifford, who bragged about being an indirect descendent of Myrtle Ricketts, the namesake of Myrtleville, would exhaust every effort to avoid getting within an arm's reach of anything that looked like work.

"Me and Hank will just have to go back there and check out that light!" Clifford said, strutting back and forth like a bantam rooster.

"No way. I'm going to listen to one of Mr. Satterly's stories, and then I'm going fishing," Hank insisted, his feet planted squarely on the ground. Of course, Hank was also looking forward to spending some time near dark-eyed Rosie, with whom he was head-over-heels in love.

He was already imagining a whole summer of being outside with Rosie, swimming in the crystal water of Honeymoon Creek — on the safe end of the creek, of course, the part that ran through Hank's farm. He also imagined getting ice cream sodas at the drugstore. And maybe even going to a street dance or two with her.

That is, when he wasn't working on his family's farm. He and his friends had just completed their first year of high school. Summer was just starting, but in typical fashion, Clifford was already squirmy and bored. And here they hadn't even been through a full day of vacation yet.

"You're scared, aren't you, Hank?" Clifford taunted.

Hank eyed him. "'Course I am. I don't know what's going on in that farmhouse, but I do know some sort of ghost has been howling over the creek, night after night, all my natural-born life. I should know — I live right across the road. If anything, she's getting worse. The old Hawkins place is on Old Man Crupp's land, back where that twisted-up creek flows through a pond."

5

Hank looked right at Clifford. "And you know how crazy Old Man Crupp is — it's like that ghost has driven him out of his mind. I think that's why he's got that bull running loose in the woods — to scare off the ghost. I'm guessing that bull's not named Lucifer because he's saintly."

Indeed, the huge white Charlais bull had once gored a man. But instead of getting rid of the animal, Old Man Crupp had fired the hand for not being able to control it. In fact, he let Lucifer run loose to keep young folks like Hank and Clifford from trespassing on his land when he wasn't able to patrol the woods and fields himself.

But it had always seemed to Hank that the bull and ghost were at odds with each other. They were foes, and strange ones at that. Lucifer had little effect on the ghost of Honeymoon Creek, his solid muscles battling a force as invisible as the very air. Yet it was almost like the essence of the ghost was constantly whistling through the bull's ears, making Lucifer as mad as Old Man Crupp. Standing out on his porch at home, Hank often heard the white bull bellow with rage in the dark woods across the road.

Thickset, in Oshkosh overalls and white t-shirt, Old Man Crupp was feared by all. He had broad shoulders and forearms like sugar-cured hams. Folks warned that if you didn't get out of his way when you passed him on the sidewalk, he'd wrestle you into a head lock and snap your neck like a toothpick. He was also bald, some people claiming that he regularly shaved his head, others that he'd once had some kind of rare disease.

But it was his eyes that bothered people the most — that wild, far-off look. Old Man Crupp regularly threatened to shoot anyone who dared set foot on his sprawling farm. As the old men who hung out on the liars' bench quipped, "You might not be dead after catching some of that buckshot in your backside, but you'd sure wish you was!"

Over the years, Old Man Crupp had amassed a small fortune, mostly from his four thousand acres of prime ground. As Hank's dad said, "Most places it takes money to make money, but around here you need *land* to make money." Unfortunately, their part of Indiana didn't have much in the way of good black dirt like across the Wabash River in Illinois. So folks had to make do with what they could get out of the pale tan soil.

Old Man Crupp worked hard, but he had never shown much sympathy for the hardships of others. Every year he'd bought up more and more of his neighbors' land, until he was the biggest farmer in the county. He lived alone, just a couple of miles off the Greenfield Slab — a "slab" in local speech was a narrow, paved country road, often just wide enough for a single car. Crupp lived in a huge brick house that was invisible from the road, sunk deeply in the woods at the end of a winding gravel lane.

Some people said Old Man Crupp had been married once but that his wife had run off on him. Others figured he had never been married. "Who'd be foolish enough to marry him?" they said.

And then there were a few folks who claimed he had done away with his wife in some dreadful fashion.

For whatever reason, an aura of mystery swirled over his entire farm: the house, barn, and outbuildings, as well the fields, pasture, and woods. Not to mention over the abandoned Hawkins Farm and that winding portion of Honeymoon Creek that flowed through his land.

Hank was both afraid of the old Hawkins place and drawn to it, seemingly against his will. He had to remind himself that it was a sweet evening in June and a good time to go fishing — or it would have been except for Clifford's annoying jabber about someone having moved into the Hawkins farmhouse.

"You said the ghost of Honeymoon Creek is a *she*," Rosie noted. "How do you know it's a woman?"

"Well ..." Hank said, reluctant to get Clifford too hopped up. "I've seen her."

Clifford scoffed, "You have not!"

Yet the girls seemed impressed. "You've really seen her?" Rosie asked.

"Yes," Hank answered, "which is why I don't want to go back there. Let's just listen to one of Mr. Satterly's stories and then go fishing down on the Wabash. I've got the worms dug, and I made some doughballs this afternoon."

"Fishing happens to be a complete and total waste of time," declared Clifford, whom folks sometimes called Bug, not so much because he resembled an insect, but because he made such a pest of himself.

Meanwhile, Mr. Satterly, whom everyone called Popper, emerged from the cafe across the street where he regularly ate his dinner. An ancient man with pure white hair and beard, he was dressed in overalls, with a plaid shirt buttoned right up to the wattles on his neck.

Hitching his thumbs in the belt loops of his jeans, Clifford urged, "Let's beat it before that ol' geezer gets over here!"

Hank stood there like an oak tree rooted deep in the earth.

Clifford grumbled, "If I didn't know better, I'd say you really liked his stories!"

Again Hank did not respond, because that was the purest truth and then some.

Most of the old men who inhabited the liars' bench — a sagging old bench located in front of Tremont's store — weren't unfriendly to young folks. But they preferred to talk among themselves. And they didn't exactly take precautions about who was standing nearby when arcing a black comet of tobacco juice in the general direction of the gutter. Mr. Satterly was the exception. He took a keen interest in young people.

As the old man tap-tapped his cane toward them, Clifford groaned, "All we ever do is hang around this boring ol' town, listening to old people. Is that all we're going to do till we get old and die ourselves? Face it, Hank, we're not getting any younger. Gosh durn it, unless we get a move on it, what are we going to tell our grandchildren? That we sat around listening to our grandparents' stories? Here we are almost grown up. And not one thing has ever happened to us in our whole entire lives! Wouldn't you like for us to have some stories of our own?"

Strangely, for the first time, Clifford Hopkins seemed to be making a bit of sense. Not much, but at least a little. Yet Hank knew better than to admit it. Besides, the two of them had already had more than their share of encounters with ghosts over the past year or so, mostly due to Clifford's passion for adventure — at least until anything scary started to happen. Then Hank always seemed to find himself suddenly quite alone.

Hank was just about to remind Clifford of that fact when Mary Ethel sang out, "Hey, I know what you guys can do. You can compromise. You can go fishing, but at Old Man Crupp's pond. That way you can explore the old Hawkins farm, too!"

"Yeah," Clifford agreed, bright-eyed as only a fool can be. "Heck, maybe we'll end up with a story that we can tell to our grandchildren someday, right here on this very same liars' bench!"

"It is odd that a light in the farmhouse has just started coming on lately," Rosie observed. "And that nobody knows the story behind the ghost of Honeymoon Creek. No one even knows how that creek came to have such a sweet and pretty name."

Hank knew he shouldn't be listening to Clifford, not for a single, solitary moment. But Rosie was a different matter. Truth be told, Hank was also curious about what was going on back there. Perhaps it was because his farm was so close by. On their side of the road, the creek ran clear and fresh, but on Crupp's land, it tore and twisted into one cutbank after another, as if it had lost its way.

Lately, feeling like the tortured part of the creek, Hank likewise had begun to wonder which way to go. He'd always wanted to be a farmer, but in the last few weeks he'd come to doubt himself. His family was having money troubles. He might not even be able to live on the land, if his family lost their farm — like so many of their friends and neighbors already had.

Some nights, as the wind sailed across the fields, he imagined the ghost howling above the creek across the road was calling him by name. But why? To draw him into her frightening world? Or for some greater purpose? He sensed that he was about to come face to face with his destiny, like a Native American youth going on a vision quest. "All right, Clifford, let's go," he said.

Clifford got wide-eyed. "You mean ... you really want to explore that old farmhouse?"

"No," Hank repeated honestly. "But if I don't go, you'll just keep pestering me all night like a mosquito, won't you?"

Clifford shrugged. "What else am I supposed to do?"

"But you've got to lead the way," Hank said.

Clifford was stung, but only momentarily. "Of course, I'll

lead," he boasted in front of the girls. "I always do. Just don't run off on me, Hank."

"Me run off? You're the one always turning tail."

"No, I'm not. You're the one who always chickens out."

Arguing between themselves, they headed to Hank's pickup. Rosie called, "You be careful back there, Hank."

"It's Clifford I'm worried about," he said over his shoulder, although truth be told, he was plenty scared himself.

"Be sure to look after Cliffie for me," Mary Ethel called to Hank.

Whirling around, Clifford pronounced, "What do you mean? It's gonna be me watching after Hank — as usual!"

Hank sighed, a calm expression on his face, although his stomach was twisting up in knots.

They climbed into his pickup, and down the Greenfield Slab they drove, the trees swirling around them and the low ground filling up with dark.

Chapter II

Quiet as his own breath, Hank slipped onto the back porch of his family's farmhouse. Collecting his fishing gear, he hustled back down the lane where Clifford was waiting for him.

Through the yellow glow of the side window, Hank had caught a glimpse of his mom and dad sitting in the parlor. She was sewing up a workshirt, and he was reading the newspaper in his favorite old easy chair. They both seemed a little older in the evening, nearer the time they'd retire from the hard work of the farm. Hank was supposed to take over the farm when he turned old enough. But lately, crop prices had been so low they didn't cover the cost of seed, fertilizer, and fuel. It was a hard time for small farmers everywhere.

Recently, his father had surprised Hank with an outright question: Did he really want to be a farmer — to take over the family farm in a few years — or not? It turned out that Hank's father had received an offer from an unnamed party to buy the farm and would have to respond, and soon.

Hank suspected the offer had come from none other than Old Man Crupp — the last person on earth Hank wanted to see end up with their farm. Hank also knew that his father wouldn't sell willingly. His family was just too far into debt. If the bank called in their loans, they'd have to sell their farm at auction — with Crupp as the only bidder. That way he'd get the farm for a song. After all, the old man practically owned the bank. Nobody would dare stand up and bid against him.

Looking both ways, the boys slipped across the Greenfield Slab, the narrow concrete road that ran in front of Hank's farm. They stopped at the barbed-wire fence, right next to the sign which read *No Trespassing*. Time and again they'd been told not to venture into those woods. "Half of Indiana is creeks and ponds," Hank's dad often told him. His mom usually added, "What's wrong with fishing in our own end of the creek, Hank? Or along the Wabash? It's dangerous in those woods. That Jake Crupp really would shoot you. And what about that ol' bull of his? Besides, you kids are always saying that creek is haunted, although how a creek so pretty can be possessed I'll never know."

This was exactly why Hank and Clifford had never dared to poke around on Crupp's land — until tonight. It was strangely quiet — too quiet — as they climbed the barbed-wire fence and crept through the woods.

"Lead away," Hank whispered.

Clifford stood there. "You go first."

"Me?"

"Yeah, you're taller. You'll be able to see the ghost better."

Hank sighed, "I knew it."

Through the congestion of leaves, branches, and logs covered with green moss, they groped their way along a deer path that followed the winding curves of Honeymoon Creek. The boys had long, whippy cane poles slung over their shoulders and a wicker tackle-box full of lead sinkers, bobbers, and extra hooks, as well as two kinds of bait — redworms dug from the compost heap out back of Hank's garden and doughballs flavored with bacon grease.

With the trees pressing in around them, they could scarcely see where they were going, and Hank was sure that Clifford would step flat-footed into a cowpie, an abundance of which were scattered through the woods. As usual, Clifford made a racket. Keeping his voice as low as possible, Hank urged him, "Walk quiet."

"I'm not making a sound," Clifford claimed as he tore through the carpet of dry leaves as noisily as a squirrel digging up acorns.

Hank whispered back, "Make much more noise and you'll wake up the dead."

Immediately, Clifford quieted down some. Whether he believed in ghosts or not, he was definitely afraid of them. As they hiked along, Hank kept alert for any sight or sound from Old Man Crupp or Lucifer — or the ghost of the creek — among the black foliage. However, the only thing he heard was Clifford snapping twigs and rustling leaves with every step he took, and complaining about all the stickers.

Clifford had always been subject to an array of fears, real and imagined — mostly the latter. Hank, on the other hand, was as able in the woods as a young bear, or at least that's what his dad said. Though not exactly unhealthy, Clifford was also burdened by a fairly continuous streak of bad luck. When they went swimming in the cool waters of Honeymoon Creek by Hank's farm, of all the kids who swam there, Clifford collected on his person the largest number of leeches. And whenever he got within a mile or so of poison ivy, he broke out in a rash and went around for a week ghost-white with calamine lotion and smelling like a hospital.

As they picked their way through the foliage, Hank could barely catch his breath, half expecting Old Man Crupp to step out from behind a tree, shotgun cradled in his arms.

"What was that?" Clifford whispered across the thickening dark.

"Nothing," Hank said. "At least I don't think so." As usual, Clifford's panic was as contagious as the measles, and Hank tingled from his fingertips to his toes.

Breaking another branch underfoot, Clifford said. "There it is again!"

"That was you," Hank sighed breathlessly.

"There's something out here!" Clifford gasped. "I just know there is. I feel it in my bones."

For once, Hank didn't argue with his friend, because he had never felt more frightened. He wished that Clifford would turn tail so that he could also flee this creepy place. But his buddy was stuck so close to him, he could have been riding in Hank's back pocket.

Sweating all over, about a mile back from the road, they finally broke out from the trees and arrived at the pond. Its surface was a dark mirror reflecting the evening sky, which was blue with streaks of purple cloud. The gray hulk of the Hawkins farmhouse loomed in the background. Fish made rings within rings in the smooth, quiet surface of the water.

"I don't care what you say, I heard something back there," Clifford muttered across the dark which was beginning to separate the boys.

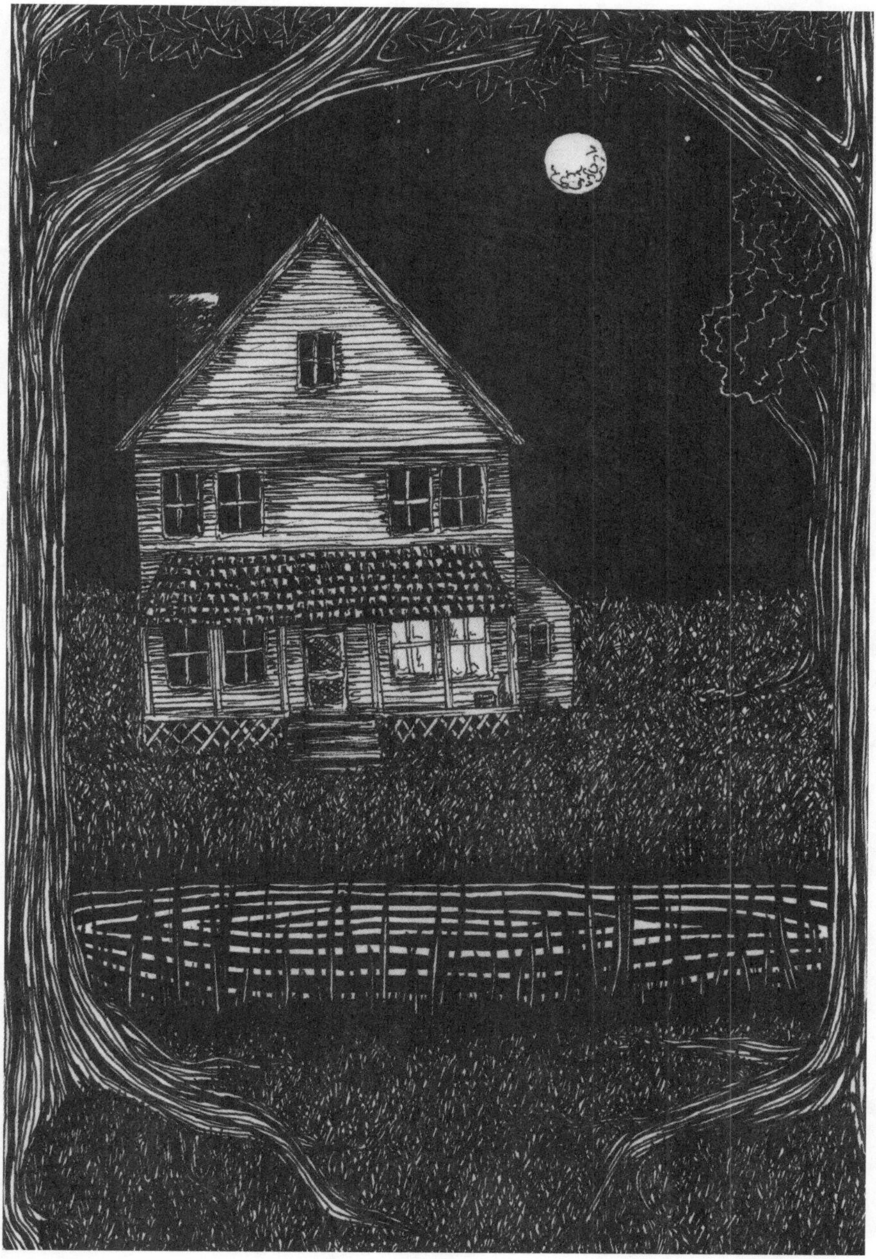

"Hush," Hank whispered. Scared or not, he had confronted few scenes as lovely and as intriguing as the one before him. He gazed across the tranquil water at the old Hawkins farmhouse, behind which the sky was darkening to purple as the sun vanished over the curve of the earth. It was all so pretty, yet sad. He wondered who had once lived there. And how the farmhouse had come to be abandoned.

Clifford whispered, "I wonder who could be holed up over there."

"Let's just leave them alone," Hank said. He knew it had to be a ghost, and he was too scared to risk rousing her. Sitting down on the bank, he squeezed a worm onto his hook and flicked his line over the rose and purple water, dropping the cork bobber in a patch of water among the lily pads.

"Hey, what are you doing?" whispered Clifford. "I thought we were going to sneak over to that old house."

"This is far enough for me. It was you who wanted to explore that old spook house," Hank said, knowing good and well that Clifford would never do anything alone, especially if it involved so much as a whiff of danger. "I'll watch from here. You go on without me."

"By myself?"

"You were the one who wanted to come here. You were bragging to the girls about how brave you are. Now's your chance to prove yourself."

Across the dark, Hank could see the whites of Clifford's wide eyes, as his skinny friend struggled to concoct his next excuse. "I would go by myself, Hank, you know I would. But it wouldn't be fair to you. You'd miss out on seeing the ghost. Besides, you need to be with me — so's I can look out for you. We'll fish for a while and keep an eye on the house all at the same time. Maybe the light will go on. Yep, that's what we'll do."

Hank hoped that they could just fish a while, then clear out before anything happened to them.

Starting out with a doughball, Clifford sat down on the bank near a sycamore tree and cast his line into the water. Hank would have reminded him that catfish didn't bite until it was good and dark, but he couldn't recall how many times he had already informed Clifford of that fact.

As they sat on the bank, Clifford glanced over his shoulder and whispered, "There could be all sorts of wild animals in these woods. Coyotes. Maybe even a bear."

Hank told him, "Lucifer's the animal that worries me the most. Not to mention Old Man Crupp."

Hank did his best to focus on fishing as, one after the other, he yanked several prime bluegill out of the water. Each fish had a bright orange belly, and gasped in the dust of the bank, its eye turned to the young moon.

Then, as the dark closed in, Hank switched to doughballs. He was a little more comfortable, because they were blending with the night as well as with the foliage around them — but mostly because Clifford had finally gone quiet.

No sooner had that thought occurred to Hank than Clifford opened his mouth again. "Know what?"

Hank groaned. "What the heck is it now?"

"I'm thinking about getting me a regular girlfriend. You know, now that summer vacation's started."

Suddenly, Hank was truly interested in what Clifford had to say. "You mean Mary Ethel Freeny, don't you?" he asked, since the two of them had been matched since kindergarten. And he'd noticed that Mary Ethel had her eye on Clifford, although for the life of him, Hank couldn't figure out why.

Clifford fumbled, "Uh, yeah, sure, I like Mary Ethel. What about you? You still like Rosie?"

"Naturally," Hank said, having been Rosie's sweetheart since first grade. He had always loved her violet eyes, her slender arms, and the delicate way she held things, as if the simplest object was worthy of close scrutiny. She had been very ill as a young child, which seemed to give her an understanding beyond her years.

Having lost her father in a car accident when she was small, she now helped her mom out in the cafe. She was a hard worker, much like Hank on his family's farm. Also, like Hank, she seemed to prefer to stand back and make a study of others, and of life in general. Lately Rosie had stirred new and confusing feelings in him, which he concluded could only be love.

And then Clifford asked, "No offense, Hank, but are you sure Rosie likes you?"

Hank threw him a fierce look. "Of course she does!"

"You know, she's a city girl."

"City girl? Myrtleville's barely a village, let alone a city," Hank noted. They had only the cafe, the drugstore, and a grocery left, along with a handful of white clapboard houses.

Clifford ignored him. "Face it, Hank, the last thing in the world Rosie wants is to end up living out on a farm."

Setting his jaw, Hank asked, "How do you figure that?"

"She wants to move away, like everybody else, to a big city. There's nothing around here any more. She told me so."

Hank didn't know why Clifford was suddenly so interested in Rosie and him. He had always assumed that Rosie and he would grow up and get married. But, he reflected, now that they were getting old enough to really be sweethearts, she might not like him anymore.

Maybe she wouldn't want to marry a farmer. Many people didn't understand farmers, and some made fun of their way of life. Others, like Clifford, even called them names — hayseeds, bumpkins, clodhoppers, and rubes.

Hank was glad when the catfish began to bite. He tried to forget everything as he pulled one glistening fish after another out of the black water. Yet he kept wondering if Rosie might want to move to the bright lights of a big city. And worrying that maybe she didn't even like him anymore.

Maybe he shouldn't become a farmer like his dad. Likely, they'd have to sell their farm anyway. But would he be able to win Rosie back, if he made other plans for his life? And he'd always loved to work outdoors.

As usual, Clifford managed to snag one or two fish. It always surprised Hank that his friend caught anything at all — but not as much as it did Clifford himself when he discovered that there was actually a small fish wriggling on the end of his line.

They continued to keep watch on the Hawkins farmhouse. However, no light went on, and as it turned out, it was the mosquitoes — Clifford swatting left and right — that finally convinced them to head for home. They had a stringer of bluegill and catfish which Hank knew he would have to clean out on their back porch, because Clifford was always so full of excuses about having a sore thumb or a kink in his elbow that it wasn't worth arguing with him about doing his fair share.

Hank was mightily relieved to be hightailing it out of there, but the moment they set out for home, Clifford got jittery again.

"What was that?" he asked suddenly.

"Nothin —" Hank stopped mid-breath, because this time he also heard a crunching sound. "Turn off your flashlight!" he whispered.

His voice getting high — even higher than it usually was — Clifford whined, "If I do, it'll be dark as sin!"

Although the faint light from the stars and moon couldn't begin to penetrate the canopy of the woods, Hank insisted, "Turn it off. So it can't see us."

Reluctantly, Clifford gave in, and the boys crept forward through the dark, listening intently. Above them, there was just a sliver of moon visible through the fluttery black leaves.

"Now I can't even see where I am," Clifford whined.

Although he was trembling all over, Hank whispered back, "Just stay calm. And walk quiet."

"How can I, when I can't even see my own nose?"

Hank figured that Lucifer wouldn't be able to see them in the dark and they just might make it out of the woods. Hearing them was another matter though — because as they stumbled along, Clifford again broke twigs and crushed leaves like he had rocks for feet.

"Walk Indian-style!" Hank urged. "On the balls of your feet. Step down easy. And just keep your head. Lucifer might not bother us unless he knows we're scared."

Suddenly Clifford screamed, "Look at that!"

Across the expanse of pasture, a yellow light flickered in a front window of the old Hawkins farmhouse.

Hank was briefly mesmerized, then the woods set to a mad howling. In a frenzy, the trees seemed to be shaking loose of their roots, and the black leaves jangled overhead. And the air was suddenly aflutter with the gauzy white form of a ghost: a woman as intangible as mist, swirling among the branches, calling out to them, "Come back. Come back. Don't leave me here!"

Hank cried, "Clifford?"

But the boy was gone. Hank glanced up, thinking the ghost had snatched his friend, but then he caught sight of him, far ahead. In a tangle of canepoles and fishing gear, Clifford was fleeing for his life down the deer trail.

Chapter III

The ghost swirled around Hank, as if she wished to snare him in the wispy white web of herself. "Don't go. Please don't leave me!" she begged.

Terror in his eyes, Clifford kept glancing back at Hank as he tore through the woods — straight into the white shadow of the giant bull, Lucifer, who blocked the path.

Gleaming in a fragment of moonlight, the huge animal aimed his powerful bulk directly at Clifford. The boy apparently heard the ear-splitting bellow just a split second before he saw Lucifer charging toward him, tearing leaves and splintering branches.

The bull caught Clifford in its horns and flung him into the air, or so Hank thought in his confusion. Actually, the flying form was the ghost, hovering over the bull who seemed crazed by her presence. And Clifford? Well, Clifford had vanished, as if snatched from the very air. Had he been kidnapped by the spirit into her invisible world, Hank wondered?

Hank scarcely had time to catch his breath, let alone try to rescue Clifford, for the bull now turned on him, snorting and pawing the ground. It was the bull's eyes that terrified Hank most. They shone with hate, driven with the need to kill and kill again. He's just like Old Man Crupp, Hank thought briefly, as Lucifer charged. Hank slipped behind a tree and the bull slammed headfirst into the trunk, gouging out bark and yellow splinters of living wood.

Hank broke a sturdy branch from a fallen tree as Lucifer charged again. Swinging the branch with all his strength, he struck the bull smack between the eyes, the wood shattering into pieces on the animal's skull. Lucifer was scarcely fazed, but the blow distracted the bull for a moment. Hank sprinted past him, racing along the edge of the creek. Out of the corner of his eye, he glimpsed something below him in the creek bed, wriggling in the mud.

"Clifford?"

"Help me, Hank!"

Sure enough, the boy had apparently stumbled backward off the cutbank and tumbled bottom-first into the creek where he was now stuck firmly in the muddy shallows. Kicking his feet and flailing his arms, Clifford screamed in panic, "He's got me, Hank! He's got me by the seat of my pants!"

Hank jumped down, grabbed his friend's right ankle, and pulled him into deeper water. Clifford looked like a scruffy muskrat as the two boys dogpaddled upstream in the deep water in the middle of the creek. The ghost hovered overhead, howling and moaning, but coming no closer. The bull crashed after them, but had no way of descending the steep bank.

When they got near the road, the boys swam under the fence that straddled the creek and slipped into the concrete culvert that ran under the Greenfield Slab. Their heads just above water, they splashed their way to the other side.

Now back within the property lines of Hank's farm, the boys climbed cautiously out of the creek and crept up to the road. Gazing into the woods across the narrow strip of pavement, Hank saw that the ghost had vanished — at least he thought so — but Lucifer was at the fence, ramming into the strands of wire mesh. The fence stretched and the posts groaned.

For a moment, Hank thought the bull would break through and come after them. But the fence held. His face now bloody, Lucifer bellowed and retreated into the woods where he took his rage out on a young maple tree.

Hank and Clifford raced up the road and across the yard to the porch of the Cantrell's white clapboard farmhouse.

Wildly panting, Clifford cried, "Lucifer got me. He got me, Hank. I'm dying!"

Hank looked him over and concluded, "He didn't so much as nick you. You just fell in the creek." However, both of them were a mess of scratches and bruises from their flight through the woods.

Terror in his eyes, Clifford said, "There's a ghost in those woods and I saw the light, too! I tell you, Hank, there is something hiding out at the Hawkins house! I told you we shouldn't have gone back there!"

Hank knew better than to argue with Clifford. Briefly, he tried to convince himself that it might have been the light of the moon glinting off a window of the farmhouse, but it wouldn't have flickered so brightly.

"Maybe it's the Leach brothers," Clifford gasped.

"Just what would they be doing back there?" Hank pondered, even as his whole body shook. Usually, the Leach brothers hung out at the Sinclair station up on Route 47 or at the pool hall over in Boggsville.

"They like to go possum hunting," Clifford said. "You know there's nothing they like to eat better'n possum. They could be cooking up a fat ol' possum back there right this very minute. Maybe they're using it as a hideout! Yep, that's exactly what they're doing."

"Nobody, even the Leaches, is crazy enough to go back there, except us."

"Maybe it's some lovebirds," Clifford speculated.

Hank shook his head. In Varnell County, there were more appealing places for lovebirds — such as cemeteries.

Clifford squirmed. "Then it must be a ghost. It just has to be! You saw her yourself. I bet they're all over the place."

"We can't say it's anything," Hank answered, his belly twisted with fear as he thought of the ghost lady hovering over his head, a vaguely human form in a long, filmy dress. For all he knew, she had been watching them the whole time. He swallowed hard. "Fact is, the only way we'll know for sure is to go back there, and have us a look."

Clifford's eyes got wide as pie tins. "Go back? Now? Are you crazy?"

"Well, you were the one who wanted a story to tell our grandchildren. You said nothing ever happens around Myrtleville. Here's your chance. Let's go back and investigate."

Clifford was struck dumb. "You don't mean you're really going to that old spook house?"

Hank wasn't sure why he felt so compelled to unravel the mysteries of the strange light and the ghost of Honeymoon Creek, even as the night deepened around them. "I've always wondered about that farm. It's such a fine old place in such a pretty spot. I can't figure out for the life of me why it was abandoned. Who would want to give up living on such a pretty little homestead on Honeymoon Creek? You coming or not?"

Clifford gulped. "Maybe we ought to wait till morning. It would be safer to explore that house in the daylight."

"Whoever's back there may be gone then. And if it's a ghost, it more than likely won't come out during the day," Hank said. "Besides, you were the one who wanted to go there in the first place."

Clifford was frantic. "Yeah, but that was before I knew there really was something back there. And what about Lucifer? He's sure enough real — he almost killed me and he'll gore you if he catches you! Let's tell Sheriff Rollins. Old Roly-Poly will know what to do. He can maybe investigate the situation."

"You know as well as me that Sheriff Rollins is afraid of the dark," Hank said. "Besides, I don't know why, but this is something I have to do."

Clifford always seemed to get Hank tangled up in various calamities, before turning tail. Yet truth be told, Hank was drawn to the abandoned farms that dotted the landscape around his home. Whenever he passed an old house or barn, the sagging timbers fading back into the earth, he wondered about its past. He listened for those voices of joy and tragedy that composed its history. So much around Myrtleville was being lost, supposedly to progress.

But Hank appreciated the past — the hedgerows clogged with pink meadow-rose, the rickety corn-cribs teetering in the sunlight, the windmills rusting in the rain, and other landmarks that told him that each of these abandoned farmhouses had a soul.

He couldn't fully explain his feelings — except that he was a young farmer himself. He had grown up part of the land. And he felt obligated to find out why ghosts had chosen to inhabit the land just across the road from his family's farm.

"You'll tell me about it tomorrow, won't you?" Clifford asked, wide-eyed, still short of breath. "If you get back alive."

"You'll have to walk home," Hank informed him.

"I can borrow your truck, can't I?" Clifford asked as he glanced around the dark.

"If you clean all these fish," Hank said, not realizing until that moment how tightly he had been gripping their catch.

"All of them? By myself?" Clifford whined. "Uh, I would, Hank, except I hurt my arm when I fell in the creek. I don't think it's broken, but it hurts something awful. It's probably sprained."

"Either clean the fish or walk home — or come with me," Hank said firmly. He might be scared out of his wits, but he wasn't about to let the fish go to waste.

Clifford must have been very frightened because, for once in his life, he didn't prolong the argument. Accepting the stringer from Hank, he hightailed it to the comfort of the light burning on the back porch of Hank's house.

In a way, Hank was thankful that Clifford was not coming with him. Slipping over the barbed-wire fence again, he crept back into the woods, glancing overhead nervously in case any of the ghosts tried to ambush him. He knew the bull was out there lurking in the dark.

And he shivered at the prospect of Old Man Crupp stepping in front of him with a shotgun pointed at his heart.

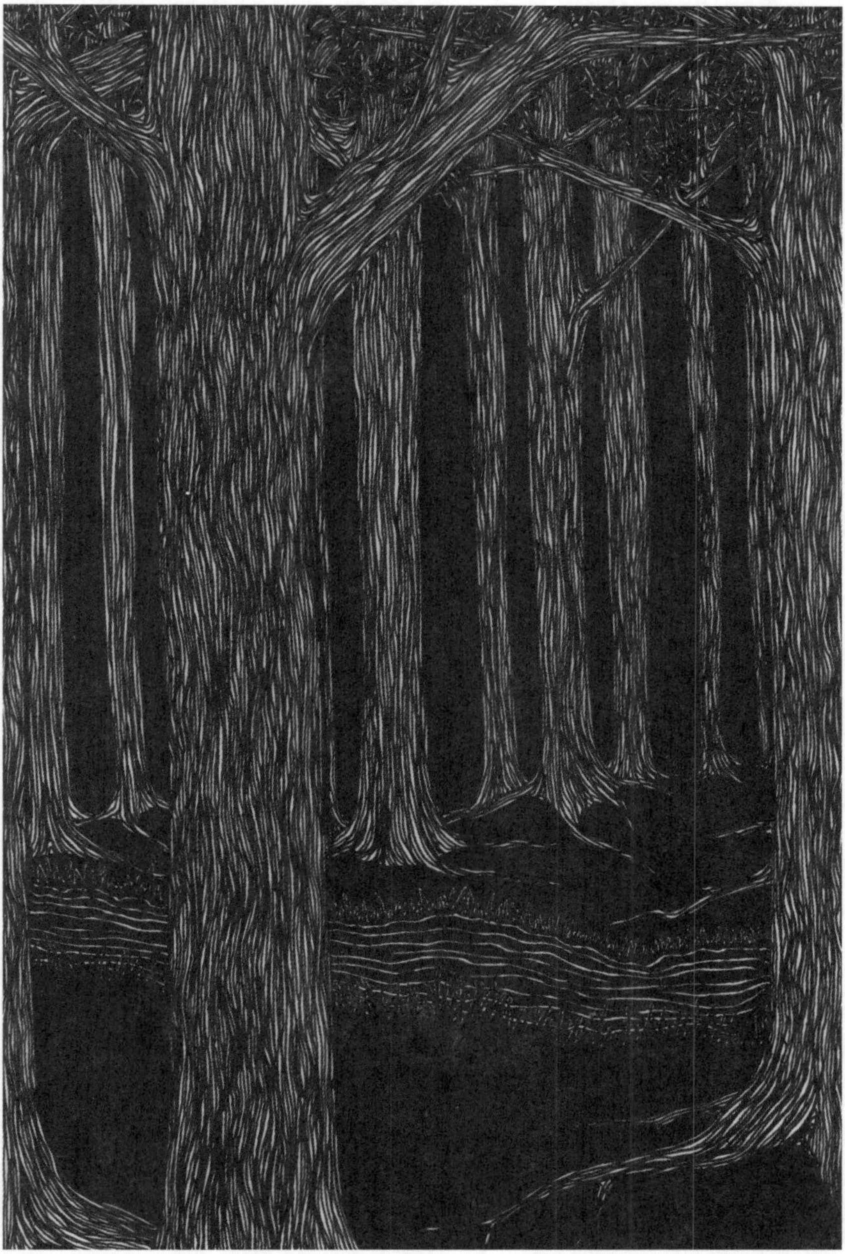

But he was filled with the need to find out just who was back at the Hawkins farm. If he kept quiet, very quiet, he just might be able to elude them all.

Breathing ever so lightly and walking ever so softly, Hank crept back to the pond.

It had become very dark, the night seeming to overpower the stars as well as the sliver of moon. He would have preferred being back home across the road, lying in the grass in his backyard, staring overhead, trying to see all the sky at once, which he knew was possible because he had done it, more than once. He simply had to look out of the sides of his eyes as well as straight overhead. That was the best part of being young, he supposed: the freedom to try most anything. He could be at ease with the world when he was outside, alone, even though he knew that when it came to the universe he was no more significant than dust.

Drawing a long breath, he turned the whole of his attention to the Hawkins farmhouse — and the single light glowing through a window just off the front porch. He couldn't see much else. So, on hands and knees, he crept across the pasture, the sweet aroma of clover in his face, the earth damp against his knees and the heels of his hands, and the crickets fiddling away, their sounds ascending high into the sky.

The tingling down his spine was just about unbearable as he crawled across the overgrown yard, pausing by the hand pump over which the windmill creaked idly in the light breeze.

As he crept to the front of the house, just under the window, he hoped that Lucifer would set upon him — to give him an excuse to flee back to the safe, predictable routines of home. But he felt deep in his soul that he had to be here. He sensed that in looking for the ghost, he was, in truth, searching for himself, although he wasn't sure how or why.

Slumping down in the weeds near the foundation, Hank paused to catch his breath. Then he rose up, ever so slowly toward the window. But even on tiptoes, stretching against the gray clapboards, he couldn't quite see into the room illumined with yellow light.

Then he noticed a milk can riddled with rust on the front porch. Ever so quietly, trembling with cold fear, he rolled it under the window. Carefully, he climbed up on it and peeked through the window. The panes were blurred with spider webs and dust, and the only light glowed from a kerosene lamp set on an old wooden table.

Everything in the house appeared to be older than his grandparents, who had passed away years ago. The place was surely a hundred years old, if a day. There were horsehair chairs and spindly-legged furniture. The flowers on the wallpaper had dulled to the blue of the sky at noon, and the woodwork had aged to a vanilla color.

At first Hank was convinced that the ancient lady steadily rocking in the center of the room had to be a ghost — the same ghost who had pursued him along the creek. Or was she? She was the spitting image, but this ghost was sun-tarnished and strong, as if rooted to the place. The ghost in the woods had appeared to be much younger, and more fragile.

Wearing a flower-print dress whose colors had faded until they were almost indistinguishable, the woman wasn't reading or knitting — just gazing into the distance, as if she were visiting a time and place deep within herself. Her white hair was pinned into a bun, and her skin was a fine netting of wrinkles.

Hank stared at her, thinking for a moment that she might be

a real person, until she turned her head ever so slowly, as if it were a thing independent of her body, and laid the fiercest green eyes upon him.

How could she have known he was there, Hank wondered? Chills flashed through him. Just barely peeking in the window, he hadn't made a sound, and he was still very much part of the night. He panicked.

Suddenly, the milk can tilted over and he tumbled to the ground, banging his shin on the lid. Though his leg throbbed with pain, he fled as fast as he could, hobbling across the yard. With every step, he could almost feel the cold hands of the ghost lady tightening around his neck.

All around him there was a mad howling, the leafy branches thrashing every which way. At the risk of running smack into a tree, he sprinted through the woods, not slackening his pace until he arrived at the fence by the road and scrambled over, scratching his left palm on the barbed-wire.

Only then did he look back and conclude that the ghost had not followed him into the velvety night. At least he thought she hadn't — yet she could be anywhere among those dark trees.

He was certain that the ghost of Honeymoon Creek was now inhabiting the Hawkins home. And deep in his bones, Hank knew that she wasn't through with him.

Chapter IV

Late into the night Hank lay awake in his upstairs bedroom, watching the flash of shadows from the maple branches blend with the flower patterns of the wallpaper. Every creak of the house seemed to penetrate him.

The Cantrells never locked their doors — in warm weather they even left them open so the evening breeze could flow through the screen doors — and he kept imagining the ghost lady drifting like mist through the screen door and right up the stairs to his room.

When at last Hank floated off to sleep, and suddenly awoke, he was jarred by the morning light. He went through chores and breakfast with his thoughts focused on what he had seen back at the Hawkins farm. He was getting ready to hill beans and potatoes in the big vegetable garden when Clifford drove into the yard, returning Hank's truck. Climbing out of the cab and rushing over to Hank, he asked eagerly, "Okay, what did you find? Come on, tell me. I can't wait to hear about it!"

Hank didn't know why Clifford, other than naturally being a

snoop, was so curious about the Hawkins farm that he would show up at his house so early in the morning. Usually in the summer months Clifford slept until well past nine o'clock, and was grumpy as a bear when his mom was finally able to roust him. But Hank knew better than to tell the blabbermouth anything about the ghost lady living in the Hawkins house, because Clifford would quickly spread the news all over the county, thick as mud in March.

Eyeing the skinny runt, Hank said, "I thought you didn't care who was hiding out back there."

"Well, I *don't* care," Clifford claimed lackadaisically, lying his heart out.

Leaning on his hoe at the edge of the garden, Hank squinted at him and suggested, "Let's you and me just forget about it then."

"Come on, Hank! You got to tell me. We're buddies."

Hank knew Clifford had some angle, so he asked him, "What makes you so all fired interested in who's at the Hawkins farm? Didn't you see enough of the ghost to suit you last night?"

"Just curious. That's all."

Hank squinted at him.

Clifford sighed. "If I tell you, you got to promise to split it with me."

"Split what with you?"

"The money! What else?" Clifford said, jumping like a cricket in the grass. "I know there's criminals back there. I'm a hundred percent sure of it. We can turn them in and get the reward. It's probably a million dollars at least. Probably more!"

Hank studied Clifford a while, not sure what to make of him — but that wasn't anything new.

Clifford rambled on, "If it's not criminals, maybe somebody's come back looking for money they hid there a long time ago. Yep, that's it! They got their life savings buried in the yard or stashed in a wall of the house. Or maybe they hid it under a floorboard. But don't worry, I'll find it."

Hank shook his head. "I just wish for once I could figure out how your mind works."

Clifford kept looking at him as bright-eyed as a pet terrier, and licking his lips like he was hoping to get a biscuit. "We'll split the reward. Or the treasure. Or whatever it is we find there. Fifty-fifty."

Hank sighed. "There aren't any criminals back there. And no hidden treasure, at least none that I know of."

"Well, who *is* holed up back there?"

Hank had a sudden feeling, almost a premonition, that he shouldn't tell Clifford about the ghost lady — if only because his friend had such a knack for messing things up. "Nobody," he said, looking away from Clifford to the green rows in his vegetable garden.

"Hank. You got to tell me! Heck, it was my idea to sneak over there in the first place."

Hank sighed again. He knew Clifford wouldn't quit bugging him until he got his way. "I'll tell you on one condition. You've got to promise not to tell a soul, least not until I figure out exactly what's going on back there. You've got to cross your heart. I know that it will be the first time in your entire life you've kept your mouth shut, but you've got to swear on your honor."

Holding his right hand up, Clifford squeezed his eyes shut and declared, "I swear to God I won't tell a soul. I swear on the graves of my ancestors, of every Hopkins and every Ricketts that's ever lived!"

Hank wasn't sure what to make of what he had seen last night. Mr. Satterly always said that the only way people knew for certain whether there were ghosts or not was when they died, which Hank wasn't in any hurry to do. So he was kind of edgy as he told Clifford, "I saw the strangest thing last night — an old lady up at the old Hawkins farm."

"What's so strange about this old lady?" Clifford asked, peering deeply at Hank.

"Her being there in the first place," Hank explained. "But mostly, she was so ancient that — well, she must be the ghost of Honeymoon Creek. She looks just like the ghost that chased us. What I don't understand is why she's started living in the farmhouse, lighting a lantern and all."

Clifford squirmed like a spider had just crawled down his neck. "Don't go saying that, Hank Cantrell. You're just trying to scare me, and it won't work."

Hank said, "I did see the ghost lady in the house, acting like she'd been living there for years. And I can prove it. We'll go back there and I'll show you."

Clifford was fairly breathless. "Now?"

"You know of any better time?"

Clifford stammered, "Uh, we could, except you know that no ghost is going to come out during the day time."

"Okay. Tonight then?" Hank suggested. "We can sneak up and peek in the window just like I did."

Clifford went silent as a fencepost, which was a rare state for him. Then, he said, "I got more important things to do than poke around some old spook house."

"Like what?" Hank asked.

"I'm not sure. But I'll think of something. Show me some

proof that there's a ghost back there, then I'll go with you."

Generally, it was Clifford who was imagining all sorts of things that weren't so, and Hank who was not believing him. Hank studied Clifford for a while, then it came to him exactly what he would do. "I can get proof," he said soberly.

"What kind of proof?" Clifford asked.

"You'll find out soon enough. In the meantime, keep quiet about the ghost lady."

"I promised, didn't I?"

Clifford turned to head back to Myrtleville on foot. Hank knew his friend was scared because Clifford didn't even whine about having to walk back to town. Hank called after him, "Hey, do me a favor, will you?"

"Favor?" Clifford asked suspiciously.

"Don't worry, it won't amount to any work for you. Just tell Rosie that I'm kind of busy today and won't be able to see her."

Clifford got a strange gleam in his eye. "Sure, Hank, any-thing you say." Then he paused in the yard, like he'd just thought of something. "Hey, Hank, I hate to be the one to tell you this, but Rosie doesn't like you anymore."

Hank just stood there, leaning on his hoe, not believing his ears.

"She didn't want to be the one to tell you," Clifford went on. "But it's like I told you, she's a city girl."

When Clifford left, Hank tried to put it out of his mind. But he and Rosie had been friends for so long. Turning back to his garden, he hilled beans and potatoes for a while, trying to feel a little more contented, telling himself not to worry about Rosie. For now, he'd just concentrate on the ghost lady.

He would show Clifford and everyone, because he intended

to take a photograph of the ghost lady. Who could ask for better proof than that? He could take the film to Tremont's Drugstore and Fountain, which would send it to Kodak and have it back in a week or so. Yet as he worked, a tear slipped down his cheek.

As the day wore on, he began to have doubts. Without a flash, his camera wouldn't work at night. He'd just have to go back that afternoon. Except that ghosts didn't usually appear in the daytime. Then he began to wonder whether the image of a ghost would even register on a photograph. It might just appear as a wisp of smoke, if anything. Finally, Hank admitted to himself that he was scared to go back there again.

He tried to convince himself that the Hawkins farm wasn't his concern — that he should go and talk to Rosie instead. At noon, he couldn't eat very much of anything. In fact, he barely finished his second helping of fried chicken, mashed potatoes, homemade noodles, green beans, kernel corn, and peach cobbler — which worried his mom because if Hank was truly dependable in one department, it was eating. He stared at his blue plate, which had a pattern of the cow jumping over the moon on it. Two seconds later, he was heading out the door.

"Where are you going?" his mother asked.

"Out to take some pictures," he said.

"That's nice," his mother smiled. "You've been working awful hard, Hank. You deserve a little time to relax and enjoy yourself."

Actually, Hank was tangled up inside. Should he really go back to the Hawkins Farm? Or should he visit Rosie? It surely wasn't sensible to be chasing after ghosts. But somehow he felt he had to see the old lady again. It had something to do with himself and his doubts about being a farmer like his father —

and maybe even about Rosie.

As he stepped out onto the porch, Hank saw Old Man Crupp. The man with his bald head and beefy arms was slowly driving by their farm in his shiny new pickup. The man didn't seem to notice Hank standing there — he was so intent upon greedily surveying the farm he couldn't wait to snatch from the Cantrell family.

Chapter V

His camera slung over his shoulder, Hank struck out for the Hawkins farm, keeping his eye out for Lucifer. Hank wasn't sure he wanted to get mixed up with the ghosts that haunted the landscape in this part of Indiana. He knew he should be content to leave well enough alone. Yet deep inside, he wanted to learn more about the history of his region. The Hawkins house, in particular, was so close to his own home. And the lazy course of Honeymoon Creek joined both farms.

However, Hank wasn't any less frightened than he had been last night. What if the ghost decided to slip through the culvert and start to haunt his own house? That bright June afternoon, as he crept through the dense green underbrush, he even hoped that he might have simply imagined the ghost lady, although that would have been one powerful vision.

Curiously, the gray clapboards of the old abandoned house appeared more ghostly in the intense light of early afternoon, sending shivers through Hank. Orange trumpets of day-lilies were clumped around the porch and the hand pump. The lawn was overgrown with Queen Anne's lace, black-eyed susans, and blue chicory. Everything was exactly as it had been the night before — the rusted windmill, the tilted porch, and those black windows staring back at him.

Suddenly, the hair rose up on the back of Hank's neck. There in the backyard, just beyond the root cellar, was the ghost lady herself bent over a hoe in the vegetable garden — or what had once been a garden, maybe a century ago. Hank couldn't imagine why she was working there, since ghosts didn't eat. At least not that he knew of. Before he could take flight, she leaned over the hoe, looked right in his direction, and yelled, "C'mere, boy."

Hank's heart was thudding hard, as though it might burst right through his ribcage. How on earth did she know I was hiding there in the bushes, he wondered? He could have run away, but he was too scared to do anything other than ease forward, keeping his distance from her.

"Didn't I see you here last night?" she asked, squinting at him, like she was taking aim.

Figuring there was no point in lying to a ghost, because they likely knew your heart and soul all in an instant, he nodded.

"You always go around peeking in other people's windows?" she asked.

"No'm. I — I was curious about who was living here. That's all," he admitted. "I didn't mean any harm by it."

"Last night I seen you fishin' over by the pond, too, with some little squirt," she said. "My land! That boy was noiser'n a flock of blackbirds in a field of ripe corn."

"That was Clifford," Hank explained.

"Is he always that talkative?"

"Pretty much."

"You live around here?"

"Yes'm."

"Whereabouts?"

"Up Honeymoon Creek about a mile. Just across the slab," Hank said politely.

There were bright sparks in her green eyes as she asked, "You mean the Anderson place?"

"No'm, it's our place. We're the Cantrells," he answered. He wondered why she would call their homeplace the Andersons'? He remembered that a family by that name had once lived there, but that was decades ago.

"I was a girl when Mr. Anderson built that house. I seen it go up with my own two eyes. Fact is, I know your father. Henry's his name, isn't it? I'd say you're his spitting image. He and your mama — Pearl — bought your place just before my husband and I sold ours."

As they stood talking, she seemed like a real person to Hank. And she did claim to know his dad. However, her clothes were so faded and her hair was so white that her whole being had an airy appearance. Yet she had tough brown hands like tree roots, and a deeply-tanned face, with wrinkles like the branches of so many rivers. Most spectacular, however, was the spark of her crisp, green eyes. Hank had never seen eyes give off so much light.

Though she appeared to have come out of another time and place, she struck him as both strong and pretty, like a weathered tree standing alone in a field. Still, he was anxious to take a photograph and hightail it out of there.

"You got yourself a girlfriend, son?" she asked casually.

Looking shyly down at the ground, he dug at a tuft of grass with his toe, gulped, and told her, "Yes. I mean, no."

She cackled. "Which is it now? Either you do or you don't."

"I mean I sort of had a girlfriend, only she didn't know it," Hank said, his voice breaking. "And now I hear she doesn't like me anymore."

Those eyes brightened more than ever. The old woman asked, "What on earth are you waiting for? If you like this girl, you ought to declare yourself."

Hank sensed that she meant no harm by her comment, but his ears warmed. He muttered, "Well, you know, I'm only fifteen years old."

"Fifteen! And here I was taking you for a full-grown man!"

Hank's lungs filled with fresh summer air. He wished for nothing more than to be a man. Having gotten his growth, he was powerfully built and tall for his age — five eleven — and he could surely do a man's work on the farm. Yet Clifford might be right about Rosie. When all was said and done, she might not want a rugged farmer with soil under his fingernails.

The old woman kept grinning away like she could see clear through him and back again. Then her eyes softened. "I was just kidding you a little about having a girlfriend," she said. "If you got one thing, it's time. Lord knows, a lot more'n me."

Hank wasn't so sure. "Why are you asking me all these questions?" he said, not to be disrespectful, but confounded that she seemed to know everything about him by simply peering into his face.

"Just making conversation," she muttered as she returned to hoeing that patch of ground. "You know, an old soul gets lonely from time to time."

Hank rubbed the palms of his hands on his jeans. "Well, I'm sorry. I didn't mean anything by it."

She smiled at him. "That's all right. Tell you what, you stick around and I'll tell you a story or two about myself. You never know, it might do you some good."

Hank edged closer. He supposed it was against good manners, even with ghosts, but he asked flat-out, "What are you doing here?"

She didn't appear offended. "Why, this here is my home, son. Didn't you know that?"

Hank sputtered, "Why — nobody's lived here for a hundred years, practically."

"More like thirty," she informed him, chuckling a little.

"Are you really putting in a garden?" Hank asked, remembering that he too had been working in his garden that day.

"Just fooling around," she explained. "I've always loved the feel of good dirt. I'm hankering to fix that coop up and get me some chickens too, if I could. I ain't ate a real egg in God knows how long."

"Real egg?" Hank asked.

"You're daggone right! When you crack 'em open, them store-bought eggs — ain't nothing but snot! There ain't no comparison with an egg from a free-range chicken with its bright orange yolk and firm whites. Here I had you figured for a farm boy."

"I am," he told her with a measure of his old pride. "And I know what you mean about those store-bought eggs. I once ate some of them when I visited my Aunt Blanche in Kokomo. They don't have any taste to them a'tall."

Glancing up from her work, the old lady asked, "Say, you want a drink of cold water? That hand pump out under the windmill still works, and the water's most refreshing. Best I ever drunk in my whole entire life."

"No'm," Hank said.

His quick answer seemed to surprise her. "Now here I figured you'd be thirsty! I know boys run themselves ragged, even in the hottest weather. Hardly nothing will ever slow 'em down. You see, I raised five boys myself. Right here in this house!"

Hank was pretty thirsty, but didn't feel comfortable enough with the ghost lady to get close enough to her for a drink of water. "Thank you anyway," he said. "But I ought to be going. I've still got chores to do at home."

"Say, what's that you got hung around your neck?" she said, as if she were asking questions just to keep him there.

"A camera."

She spat into the warm gray dirt at her feet. "Never had much use for one myself. All I ever cared to remember I've kept right up here in my old noggin." She tapped the right side of her head with her bony forefinger. "There ain't nothing better in this world than a good memory. You remember that, son."

"Yes, m'am."

She chuckled at her little joke. As Hank eased away from her, she said, "Sure you don't want to sit down and visit for a spell?"

"I really got to be going," he said.

"I ain't gonna bite you, if that's what you're afraid of."

"Like I said, I got my chores to do."

She shrugged. "I'd never keep a man from his work."

Secretly, not bringing it up to his face, he aimed the camera at her, and as he backed away from the ghost lady he squeezed the shutter button.

She called after him, "Say, boy, you got yourself a name?"

"Yes, m'am," he hollered back. "Hank." Tinged with a blend of pride and uncertainty, the sound of his name seemed to ring through the woods and pasture.

"You got a last name?"

"Cantrell."

"That's right. You're the Cantrells. I knew your father when he was yet a young man. I sure hope he doesn't sell your farm, especially not to that pig-eyed Crupp. Come again, Hank Cantrell. You're welcome anytime. You know, it's good to know a neighbor."

"I will," he answered, because he liked the old lady, even if she was more than likely a ghost. But how on earth did she know that his father was thinking of selling their farm?

Chapter VI

The next evening, as soon as he was done with his work, Hank walked out of the barn and stopped in his tracks. There across the yard and strawberry patch was Old Man Crupp leaving the house. His dad followed the heavy-set man onto the side porch where they stiffly exchanged goodbyes.

Hank had never made a thorough study of Old Man Crupp, but for some reason, ever since the talk about the light in the window of the Hawkins farmhouse had begun to circulate around town, the man had seemed agitated. Now he seemed even more anxious than ever to possess the Cantrells' farm as quickly as possible.

Briefly, their eyes met across the wide expanse of the yard — the old farmer and the young man — and Hank refused to look away. Old Man Crupp's face finally broke into an ugly grin, as though he knew that he had the upper hand and there wasn't anything Hank or his father could do about it. Then he swaggered over to his truck, cocksure and mean as always — yet with a curious glimmer of hesitation in his eye. But why?

Surely, he wasn't afraid of Hank. And it couldn't be guilt — the man had never shown the least shame. Young as he was, Hank knew that people like Crupp feared only one thing — getting caught. Everything Crupp had ever done was wrong, but it wasn't illegal, at least as far as anyone could prove. So what could be bothering him?

Whatever the case, Hank was glad to see the man gone. He tried to put Old Man Crupp out of his mind as he slipped down the tractor lane, making a big loop of their farm.

On either side of him, the corn was just inches high, its small leaves fluttering tender green. Usually he loved those sweet afternoons in June, with the blue sky overhead reaching into infinity, the wind flowing over him, and the thin lines of corn like delicate stitches tracing the brown folds of their land.

Ahead of him, mourning doves splashed around in dust baths. At his approach, they whirred into flight, so swiftly that they seemed to take his breath away with them. Yet Hank felt uneasy. He was being devoured by something from the inside. What would he do with himself, if they could not keep their farm? And what was he doing chasing ghosts, when he should be looking for some way to save their homeplace?

Cutting across the Greenfield Slab, he climbed the barbed-wire fence and soon was in Old Man Crupp's pasture, about a quarter of a mile from his house. He looked every which way for Lucifer. A few Hereford cows were casually grazing up the slope toward a hedgerow, but the bull wasn't among them.

Hank felt fortunate not to encounter the bull in the open field. But he wondered when his luck with Lucifer would run out. He knew the bull was out there, brooding and hostile — perhaps hidden in the dense foliage of the woods, eyeing him at

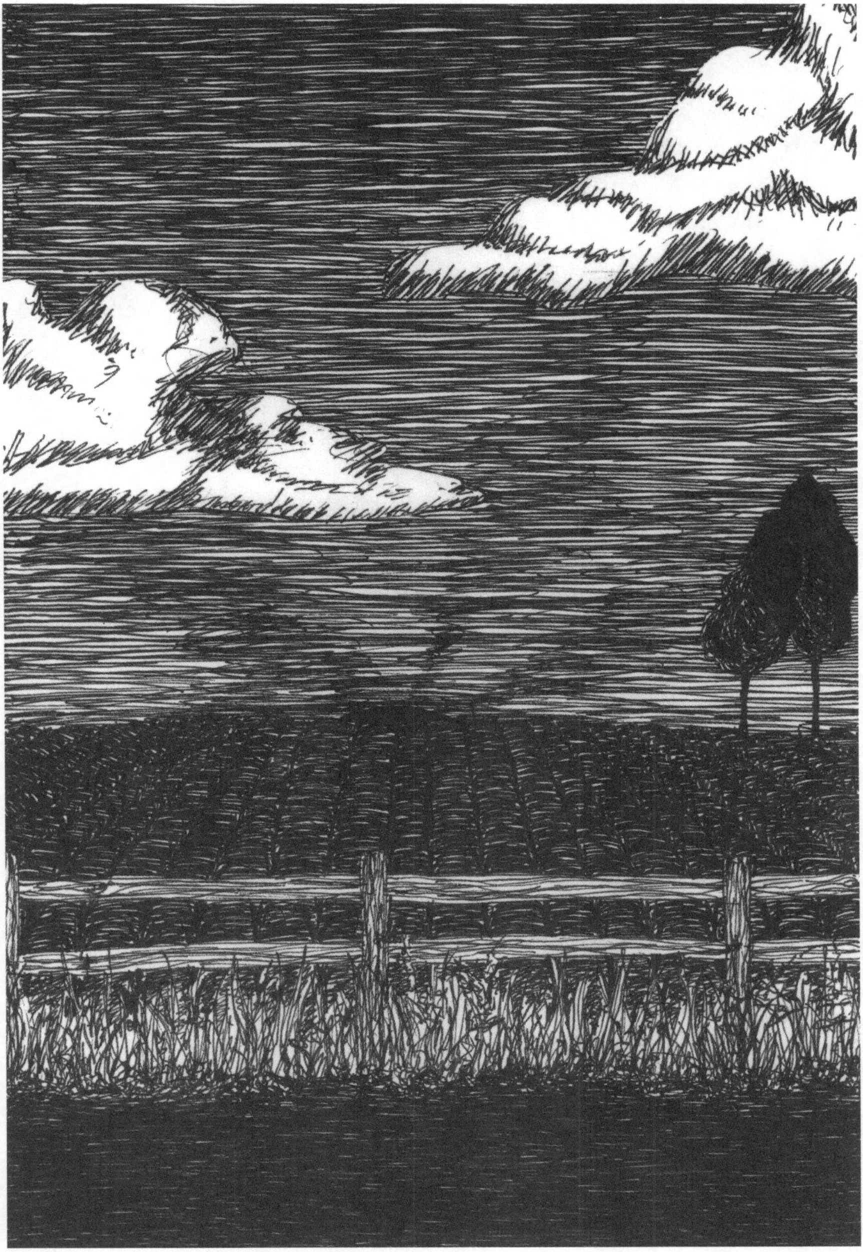

that very moment. Dodging cowpies abuzz with blue-bottle flies, he waded through the grass, on edge, toward the Hawkins farm.

From a distance Hank caught sight of the ghost lady sitting on the porch, rocking away. And if he wasn't mistaken, her face lit up at the sight of him.

"Howdy-do, boy!" she said as he hiked through the Queen Anne's lace in the yard.

"'G'afternoon," Hank said, flagging his arm, like he had just happened by, when in actuality he had made a beeline for her farm.

"One heck of a pretty day," she observed. "Makes a body glad to be alive."

Hank tensed. "Alive?" He hadn't meant to let the word slip out.

The ghost lady's white eyebrows wriggled like caterpillars. "Yessir. What do you think?" Then she rocked back and laughed so openly that Hank could see the gold in her teeth. "You didn't think I was a ghost or something, did you, son? My land, do I look that old?"

"No, ma'm," he rushed to say, although she did indeed look old enough. "It's just that, well, you appeared here out of no-where."

"Come up on this here porch, Hank Cantrell," she said, extending her forearm. "Lay your hand right here." Hesitantly, Hank stepped onto the rickety porch. Standing right next to the lady, he placed his hand on her arm. Her skin felt soft and loose, and slightly cool to the touch, as well as a bit dry. "I'm pretty well wrinkled up," she cackled. "But I'm still here in the flesh. Or what's left of it, although Lord knows I've been on the scrawny side most all my life!"

For a moment they peered at each other. Hank felt foolish for thinking that she might be a ghost — but she had to be the ghost of Honeymoon Creek he'd seen the other night, as well as occasionally over the years since he was a boy. Puzzled, he asked directly, "What's your name?"

Her eyes getting sparkly again, she said, "Why, Bonnie's my name. Bonnie Hawkins."

"Hawkins? You mean this is your place?"

She clamped her jaws together and nodded resolutely, as she told him, "It was our farm once upon a time."

"But what are you doing here now?"

"My, you're full of questions today, ain't you?"

Hank shrugged. "I was just wondering. That's all. Besides, you asked me plenty of questions yesterday."

"Fair enough," she said, rocking a little faster so that the whole porch seemed to creak in rhythm with her. "You asked what I'm doing here so I'll tell you. I live here, son."

"You did once," Hank pointed out. "But this isn't your land now. You've got no right being here."

Cocking an eye at him, she snapped, "I'd say I got about as much right being here as you do!"

"You've got me there," Hank acknowledged. "But I'm just visiting, sort of. It seems to me that you've gone ahead and moved in."

Staring off into the distance, she said, "Is that a fact now?"

"It most positively is."

"Supposing this ain't my land — which I'll allow you it ain't. Not by law," she said. "But let me ask you, just who am I hurting by being here?"

Hank shrugged. "Nobody that I can think of."

Nonetheless he wanted to warn her about Lucifer — that old bull would toss her around like a rag doll if he got hold of her — and tell her how Old Man Crupp would surely have her removed, literally thrown off the property, if he found her living back here.

The light in Bonnie's eyes intensified. "You know the old Jenkins' place?"

Hank was puzzled. "No'm."

"Up by the crossroads! You know where you drive around that big ol' burr oak tree that sits practically in the road? That big brick house?"

"You mean the Lovingtons'?"

She waved him off. "They might be living there now. But the Jenkins was them who built it. Don't you know none of the history hereabouts, sonny? That's where my Lester growed up." Hank stood there, not sure what to make of her. She must have seen the questioning look in Hank's eyes, because she said, "You sit yourself down next to me, Hank Cantrell. I'll tell you a story that might do you some good, and then some."

Sitting down on a square-back chair, Hank was right next to her, so close that she could have touched him. She had such a glow about her that he liked the feeling of being near her.

"I was sixteen years old when it happened," she began. "Lester and me had been in love for going on a year. Problem was my dad didn't take to Lester. Said he was a no-account. So you know what we up and did?"

"No'm."

Her eyes shone like the rippled light on the creek when a soft wind was blowing over the water. "We eloped. You know what it means to elope, Hank?"

"Yes, m'am. Not first hand, that is."

68

She chuckled, "I suppose not. Anyways, my dad wouldn't allow me to marry Lester, no two ways about it. But Lester was headstrong and, truth be told, so was I.

"We'd sneak out to see each other most every night, but there weren't hardly enough time for us to be together. So one night Lester he says, 'I'm just about ready to do it. How about you, Bonnie?'

"Well, I said yes quicker'n you can blink your eyes. I'd been pretty much ready all along. You see, my Lester wasn't handsome — Lord no! — not with them big ears of his and that nose growin' like a sweet potato out of his face. But he was a good-hearted boy, and a hard worker.

"The very next night he hitched up his dad's buggy and drove over to my house. I lived over on Highland Road. You know where there's a little rise to the land, and a grove of sassafras trees? The house was knocked down years ago, and the land's all in corn and beans now.

"You wouldn't even know a farm was once there, but that's where I was born and raised. I could go by there right this very minute and tell you exactly where the house, the barn, the chicken coop, garden, strawberry patch, and everything else was situated.

"Anyways, Lester he left that buggy a quarter mile down the road from the house. It was well past midnight and we did have a dog, but ol' Spangles liked Lester and didn't bark at all when he come into the yard. Lester snuck around back of the house and climbed the lattice to the back porch roof, and there I was waiting by my window.

"First thing he said to me was how pretty I looked in the moonlight. I surely had no trouble getting out of there.

"Truth be told, I'd climbed down that lattice any number of

times before to visit with Lester. If I close my eyes, I can still smell the honeysuckle like it was yesterday.

"And there you have it. Lester and me drove over to a justice of the peace in Boggsville, name of Amos T. Freeny. Lester give him two dollars — a lot of money back then — and he married us right on the spot. Lester and me went back to our own home. And you know where that is, boy?"

Hank shook his head.

"Right here!" she said, sweeping her arms over the land around them. "Right here where we're a-sittin'." She leaned back and rocked a while, thinking, with a wrinkly smile on her face.

"Lester's dad give him this house along with 160 acres to make good on. It was half his farm, but Lester was his only son. Of course, it weren't as pretty then as it is now, but we worked hard and turned it into a right good farm.

"Now my dad, he wouldn't talk to me for a year after Lester and me got married. He'd let me visit at home, after a while, but it was nigh on two years — I had one baby and another on the way — before he set foot in our house. But he come around, eventually. He had to, for it was a good marriage.

"Over the years Lester and me added on to the house and built up the farm. Then Lester got drafted and he went off to fight in Europe in World War I. They called it the Great War, though I never seen anything so great about it. Never thought I'd ever see him again. Seems like everybody in that war either got killed or had an arm or a leg blowed off.

"But Lester he wrote pretty regular. We had us three children by then, all boys. Me and Lester wasn't ones to waste time. Never could come up with a girl, though, hard as I tried. But I took care of them boys and this here farm all by myself."

She quieted down briefly, still rocking away, then nodded to her left. "You see that field over there, Hank? When my Lester was gone to war I worked it for three seasons — plowing, planting, cultivating, and harvesting — with nothing but a cantankerous old mule name of Ebenezer to help me.

"It weren't easy, not by a mile. But we didn't have no choice. We couldn't afford to hire a hand, even if a fit man could've been found this side of the Atlantic during the war. My dad had passed on. And Lester's dad he was gettin' up in years and couldn't hardly keep up with his own farm.

"If I didn't bring in a crop each of them years we'd've lost the farm, and then what would my Lester have come home to?"

She spat into the grass just off the porch and went on, getting more than a little hot. "Old men used to drive by in their buggies — rich men from town, bankers and what not — on a dirt road that used to wind past the field right over there.

"They'd stop at the side of the road, and shake their heads at me working that field. They said a woman couldn't do that kind of work, that I'd break down. When I showed them I could, they said a woman shouldn't doing that kind of work, that it weren't proper.

"The way they gossiped, like a bunch of old crotchety hens!" She leaned back and laughed, "Well, I showed 'em.

"Lester finally come back from that fool war, alive and not missing any bodily parts, which was a miracle in and of itself. When all was said and done, we had us five boys.

"All them years we made just one mistake — other than Lester's going off to that war, which he didn't really have much choice about, on account of his being drafted. Our mistake was leaving this farm.

"Actually, when it come right down to it, we didn't have much choice about that either. We got squeezed off this land and cheated at the same time.

"And you can guess who done it."

Chapter VII

Hank figured that Bonnie had pretty much forgotten about him, until she leaned forward and looked directly into his face. "Let my story be a lesson to you, Hank Cantrell. There ain't nothing that can replace living on the land.

"To know it's there each morning when you wake up. To feel it warm on the bottoms of your bare feet, to see it turn dark when the rain comes down. To smell its sweet aroma when you're plowing in the spring. You think many farmers these days stop to crumble the soil through their fingers? No sir, not with the chemicals they're dousing it with. You know, we never had much need for chemicals and such on our land, not if you follow sound practices and ain't afraid of a little work."

"That's how I'd like to farm," Hank said, his voice trailing off. "If I can...."

"You got to love the land like a wife loves a husband," Bonnie went on. "'Course, Lester said it was just the opposite — like a husband looking out for his wife. But it all adds up to the same thing, Hank. And when you decide to farm you're making a vow with the earth to work together, to respect each other and look out for each other. Seems like the earth is always more than willing, if you treat 'er right."

She stared off into the middle distance. "Lester and me put too much trust in other people, I suppose. We did walk away with enough money to buy us a little house in Boggsville. But I tell you, Hank, it weren't never the same. And you know what? We didn't have to sell this farm. We was misled and cheated."

For the first time since he had met her Hank saw the light go out of Bonnie's eyes. "This here is where we belonged all along, and it got took away from us by a sneaky, lowdown crook who already had more money and more land than he knew what to do with."

Hank wanted to ask her many things, mainly why had she been drifting over the creek all these years? He could have sat and listened to her for the rest of the afternoon. Her stories were as good or better than Mr. Satterly's — and hers were even true. Yet he felt obliged to ask, "What brings you back now, and how did you get here?"

The old woman sighed. "Why? Well, I'd say I come back in the first place to remember. You see, this is my first year without Lester, and we're coming up on our seventy-fifth wedding anniversary. I wanted some time to sit and visit with my memories."

Her eyes had a steely glint. "And in the second place, I got me a little matter that needs to be settled."

Not sure what to make of her remark, Hank asked, "How long do you figure on staying here?"

Setting her jaw, she said fiercely, "For as long as it takes!"

He felt obliged to tell her, "The man who owns this land — Old Man Crupp — he's more than mean. He's also got a bull named Lucifer that he sets loose on people."

"You think I don't know that pig-eyed Crupp?" Bonnie snapped. "Who do you think cheated Lester and me out of our farm? It was the very first piece of ground that crook bought up hereabouts, going on thirty years ago. I'm surprised his father let him do it — but then his father up and died, so there was no one to stop him. But now we got to keep him from buying any more, including your farm, Hank!"

Hank was stunned. "Stop him? How?"

"Don't you never mind how," she said. "Even if we have to move heaven and earth, we've got to do it." She snorted. "I know that pig-eyed man is gonna try to run me out of my own home — even though I don't expect to be here for more'n a short little visit and I don't have another home nowhere else on this green earth. He's already done it once, but he won't get away with it again. He made Lester and me feel we weren't no more impor-tant than dust."

"But you can't stay here," Hank said. "He'll find out, and knowing him he'll have you put in jail for trespassing. And what about Lucifer, that bull of his?"

"Truth be told that bull worries me some, and I'd advise you to walk careful. That bull is as loco as Old Man Crupp himself. But I ain't going to no jail, least not for some piddly little crime like trespassing," Bonnie declared. "If I got to go to jail, it's going to be for a major crime."

"What do you mean?" Hank asked, suddenly short of breath.

Staring off into the blue sky, she reflected, "It was just last winter that my Lester died, and it come to me that one of these days I'm gonna pass on, too. So's I decided it was high time to come home for a visit before it's too late. I found out what Crupp has done, and it's a sight worse than cheating people out of their homes. Tomorrow it'll be me and Lester's anniversary, which I plan to celebrate right here. And then we'll take care of that pig-eyed Crupp. I admit that he's got all the laws of the land on his side, but that don't matter to me no more."

"But what'll you do if Old Man Crupp shows up?" Hank asked. "He's got a gun."

She snorted. "And you think I don't? Now, only weak folks and cowards need guns. But a body has a right to defend herself in some fashion. When he shows up, he'll have a little surprise waiting for him. And it'll be loaded!" She let loose with a cackle of a laugh. And gave Hank a wink.

"But for now, nobody except you and me knows I'm here, Hank. So I've got just one favor to ask of you. Don't tell a soul that I'm back here. I don't want to get ambushed. I aim to enjoy me and Lester's anniversary in peace. Then you and me can take care of that Crupp, for all time. Can you promise me that?"

"Yes'm," Hank said, although he immediately thought of Clifford. His friend had sworn not to spill the beans to anyone, but Clifford had the most active mouth in the county.

Besides, he was still not sure who Bonnie actually was. Was she real? Or was she the ghost of Honeymoon Creek, who had been haunting the waters for as long as he could remember?

He blurted out his question, "Wasn't that you that chased Clifford and me away from the creek last night?"

Tears welled in Bonnie's eyes. "No, son, that poor soul is the ghost of Angie Crupp. If you think Crupp was rough on his neighbors, you should have seen how he treated her, his own wife, that frail, broken-hearted woman."

"I heard she ran off on him," Hank said.

A strange look darkened Bonnie's face. "Not hardly. Crupp had to own everything, even her. He never let her go."

"Well, she vanished. Years ago," Hank said.

Bonnie stared at him, a torn look in her eyes. "That's what I thought, or tried to tell myself all these long years. But I found out the truth just the other day," she said. "Old Man Crupp murdered her."

"How do you know that?" Hank asked, short of breath.

"I can't go into the particulars, but I spoke with her the other night," Bonnie went on. "You see, Angie was my baby sister."

Hank was stunned. So that explained the odd resemblance between Bonnie and the ghost of Honeymoon Creek. "I thought you — you might be her."

"We were as close as sisters can be," Bonnie explained. "My dad often said we were like two peas in a pod. Even though she was a lot younger than me." Her eyes softened. "I see her every night, floating up out of the gloom. Her face is clear, but her eyes have a terrible look to them.

"She's trapped here, Hank, and I need you to free her and bring that pig-eyed Crupp to justice. I'm an old lady and there's only so much I can do, whereas you're a strapping young man. We don't have much to offer you, but if you succeed, I'll promise you one thing. You'll save your farm and you'll be rewarded handsomely. Can you help me, son?"

Although he wasn't sure what he could possibly do, Hank readily agreed. "Of course I will, but what exactly do you want me to do?"

"I'll tell you tomorrow. For now, I just want to celebrate me and Lester's anniversary in peace."

Thinking of Clifford, Hank became anxious all over again.

Quickly saying goodbye to Bonnie, he hurried back home, intent upon finding his talkative friend to remind him to keep his big mouth shut.

But as he crossed the Greenfield Slab and hiked up the lane, there was Clifford, standing on their back porch, just in time for supper. Suddenly, Hank was overwhelmed with the darkest sense of foreboding.

Chapter VIII

As he approached the porch, Hank was about to remind Clifford to keep quiet about Bonnie when his mom appeared behind the screendoor. "Why, Clifford, what a surprise! You're just in time for supper," she said, bright as can be.

"I am? Oh, mercy me," he answered, acting innocent, as if he didn't know good and well that it was suppertime.

Hank recalled how Clifford often bragged about how his mom fed him TV dinners and other storebought food — like frozen waffles — that only took a few minutes to heat up. However, he ate at Hank's house as often as possible. Apparently those packaged dinners weren't all Clifford had them cracked up to be.

Passing the mashed potatoes, his mom mentioned, "I heard there's somebody living back at the old Hawkins Farm."

Oh, no, Hank thought. It was supposed to be a deep secret. He glanced at Clifford, who pretended to be so fascinated with his mashed potatoes that he couldn't take his eyes off them.

"I doubt it," Hank's dad answered, stabbing a piece of roast beef. "Jake Crupp would have run 'em off in two seconds."

Although Hank had proof right inside his camera — once he took the film to the drugstore and got the pictures back — he didn't offer any comment.

"But there is! It's a crazy old lady," Clifford erupted, as though the words were just bursting to get out of him. "She's living in that old farmhouse on Old Man Crupp's land. Everybody knows about it."

"What do you mean everybody?" Hank demanded, squinting at him across the expanse of the table. "It was just yesterday ..." He cut himself off as he noticed his dad staring at him.

"Everybody knows all about her," Clifford went on with an air of authority. "'Cept you, Hank. And you're the one who's been snooping around there practically day and night."

Hank's dad laid his arms on the table and asked Clifford, "Just what are you talking about, young man?"

"Hank thought there was a ghost living up there," Clifford blabbed a mile a minute, like his tongue had come completely loose. "He really did! That's what he told me. He thought the old lady was a ghost!"

"I thought *maybe* she was a ghost," Hank explained. "I wasn't certain."

Putting down her fork, his mom said, "I don't think you should be going over there, Hank."

His dad added, "Crupp will shoot you, if he catches you on his land, Hank. I wouldn't put anything past that man."

Hank wanted to tell his parents about Bonnie — and about the murder of her sister Angie — but he had promised to keep quiet. However, Clifford couldn't keep quiet for two seconds.

"I told Hank he was trespassing," Clifford rattled on. "I told him he shouldn't be going back there!"

Hank could have reminded Clifford that he was the one who wanted to go to the Hawkins Farm in the first place, but what was the use? His slippery sidekick would just dream up another convenient excuse and wriggle out of the least little bit of responsibility.

"Who is this old lady?" his mom asked, gazing at Hank with those powder-blue eyes of hers.

"I heard she broke out of a loony bin," Clifford rushed to say. "She's cuckoo is what I hear. Why else would she be holed up on Crupp's land?"

That got Pearl Cantrell's attention. Turning to Hank, she said, "You hear that, son? This could be a dangerous situation."

"I doubt whether this gossip is true," Hank's father said. "You ask me, there's nobody there. We've heard stories about that creek being haunted for years — when most likely it's just a wisp of fog drifting over the water. Now people think they see a light in a window, and it grows into another tall tale. It's amazing how that kind of talk gets around, until people begin to believe it, especially when ol' Clifford here is talking his head off."

"But people've seen her," Hank's mom said. "At least that's what I've heard."

"Who?" Henry Cantrell asked.

"Well, there's that light in the window."

"See what I mean? That's probably just a reflection of the moon in a window of that old house."

As Hank pushed away from the table, his mom asked, "You skipping dessert, Hank?"

"I'm not hungry anymore," he said, glaring darkly at Clifford.

His dad called after him, "Where you going, son?"

"Outside."

Hank and his father gazed steadily at each other. I am like my father, Hank thought, at least when he was my age. But will I be like him when I am his age — a lean, sun-tarnished farmer in faded blue jeans and chambray shirt, walking my own pasture as one season unfolds into another?

As he made for the door, Hank knew deep in his soul that he had to trust Bonnie and help her, as she had asked. It might very well be the key to his own future.

But what could she have in mind? Somehow they'd have to prove that Old Man Crupp had murdered his wife. Then the old farmer could be sent to prison.

But the Cantrells still wouldn't have any money. And they would still have to sell their farm, even if it wasn't to Crupp.

Letting the screen door slap behind him, Hank wandered out into the backyard. Not two seconds later, Clifford caught up with him and asked, "Hey, where are you going in such a hurry?"

Hank whirled on him. "Nowhere with you, not with your big mouth."

"Hey, I didn't mean nothing by it," Clifford said. "It just kind of slipped out. It was an accident."

"You swore on the graves of your ancestors."

"No, I didn't."

"Yes, you did!"

"Well, maybe I just had my fingers crossed." Without giving it another thought he blabbed away, "I hear that old lady is really weird looking — all dressed up in old-timey clothes."

Hank stuck his hands on his hips. "Now who did you hear that from?"

Clifford sagged. "I'm not sure."

"It wasn't anyone who's really seen her, because she wears

regular old clothes like any farm woman," Hank said firmly. "Just who did you tell about the ghost lady?"

Clifford shrugged. "Just one or two people. Maybe a few more. Well, after a while I kind of lost count. But they all promised to keep quiet. Honest they did. I made them swear, just like you made me. At first, nobody knew a blamed thing about her. Now everybody's so interested in her they can't hardly stand it."

"Gosh darn it," Hank muttered, furious at himself for setting off this gossip. Old Man Crupp would surely find out soon enough, if he didn't already know, and then he'd go after Bonnie, spoiling her anniversary, which meant Hank had to act, and fast.

Clifford licked his lips. "I'm not 'sposed to tell you this, Hank, but since we're best friends, I will. The Leach brothers are going to get her tonight."

Since dropping out of high school (already more than a few years behind schedule), the Leach brothers — Orville, Junior, and Ferris — had hung around Myrtleville, having nothing else to do. Occasionally they picked up odd jobs as farm hands. But for the most part they idled away their time fiddling with the old cars that accumulated in their yard because they could never get any of them running. Individually they were plenty stupid. But when the three of them got together, they were even dumber, and more dangerous.

"What are they going to do?" Hank asked.

"They're gonna run her off."

Hank ground his teeth. "What for?"

"Just for the heck of it. Besides, they figure Old Man Crupp will give them some kind of reward, if they get rid of her without him having to go to the sheriff and all."

"Exactly when are they going back there?" Hank asked.

"I'm not supposed to tell. I swore I wouldn't. And you know me. I never break an oath."

Hank glared at him, hard.

"As soon as it's dark!" Clifford squealed.

Having started this gossip, Hank felt obliged to help Bonnie, but what on earth could he do?

Chapter IX

Before he ventured into those haunted woods again, Hank wanted to ask the advice of Myrtleville's oldest and wisest story-teller, Mr. Satterly. Abandoning Clifford in the yard, Hank climbed into his pickup and drove into town.

Peeking through the plate-glass window with "Courtesy Cafe" painted in swirling letters overhead, he spied Mr. Satterly at his usual place. As he had expected, the old man was drinking root beer and telling a whopper, judging from how animated he was, his arms gesturing this way and that.

Rosie was wiping down the counter, and she looked as pretty as ever, but also tired from her long day at work. Her hair was put up with bobby pins, but a few strands had come loose and fluttered about her neck and forehead. As Hank strode into the cafe, he wanted to say a word to her, but she turned away, like she couldn't stand the sight of him.

So Clifford was right, he thought. She really didn't like him anymore. Hank was broken up inside, so much in love with her. But at the moment, he was also entangled in this situation with

Bonnie and whatever else was out there in the woods and fields. Holding back his feelings, he approached white-haired Mr. Satterly as the old man concluded his story.

"Can I talk to you, Popper?" he asked soberly.

"Well, pull up a chair and fire away!" the old man boomed.

"It's private," Hank told him.

Of course, that instantly drew the attention of everyone within earshot, which didn't bother Mr. Satterly in the least, because he always liked to be in the spotlight. Yet the old man could see the hurt in Hank's eyes. Hoisting himself up from his chair, he exhaled. "Let's you and me go out to the liars' bench." Gripping the polished handle of his cane, he tottered toward the door.

Hank glanced at Rosie again, but she was devoting her full attention to rinsing soap suds off some water glasses. How could it be over with her, before they had really even gotten started? He wished he could at least understand what had gone wrong. Turning his back to Rosie, Hank walked with Mr. Satterly down the street. They sat down on the liars' bench in front of Tremont's Drugstore and Fountain.

"It's about an old lady I met," Hank told the man as soon as he settled himself on the bench. "You probably knew her. She's from around here, or at least she used to be. Her name is Bonnie Hawkins."

Mr. Satterly's white eyebrows furrowed. "So you're the one spreading those stories about Bonnie."

Hank shook his head. "No, sir, that's Clifford."

Mr. Satterly snorted. "Clifford, huh? I should've known."

"I just met her yesterday," Hank explained. "But I really like her and, well, I heard tonight the Leach brothers are going up there to run her off."

Mr. Satterly stared hard at Hank. "Son, I knew Bonnie Hawkins, which would put her well into her nineties now, if she was still alive."

"Still alive?" Hank echoed. "I think there's some mistake, Popper. She's alive, and then some. I've seen her with my own two eyes."

Mr. Satterly scratched his beard. "I thought I heard she had passed on not long ago. 'Course, I could have gotten some incorrect information. Around here, you hardly know who to believe sometimes. You say she's living on her old homestead?"

"Yes, sir. But just sort of visiting."

"She moved away years and years ago. I remember that well," Mr. Satterly recalled, glancing down at his gnarled hands resting on the curve of his cane. "You see, I once carried a torch for Bonnie Hawkins. 'Course just about every young man hereabouts had his eye on her. She had a fierce beauty about her that's hard to put into words. And an independent spirit."

He spoke as if drawing the memories from the mist of the distant past. "I was surprised old Crupp got the best of her and Lester when they sold that land. They always claimed he tricked them, that they didn't sell willingly. But it was never proved, and I never really knew the particulars of it."

Although he was the best storyteller in the county, Hank knew that Mr. Satterly could keep a secret when he had to, so he explained about Bonnie — and her murdered sister, the real ghost of Honeymoon Creek.

"We never could figure out why Angie married that lowdown Crupp, or why she vanished," Mr. Satterly reflected. "But that might very well explain this whole sad situation, though it all seems pretty far-fetched. Hank, are you sure you're not making all this up out of your head?"

"No, sir," Hank answered. "You know me, Popper, I wouldn't do anything like that."

"You wouldn't, son, but how 'bout Clifford? He sure as heck would."

"Well, he did squeal to the Leach brothers," Hank said. "And Lord knows what else he's been spreading around town."

Mr. Satterly sighed. "Those Leach boys are so stupid they'll likely hurt her. Maybe we ought to call Sheriff Rollins. But then he'd have to remove her from the property himself."

"It would be great if she could just stay one more day," Hank explained. "You see, tomorrow's her wedding anniversary."

Mr. Satterly rubbed his chin. "If I was a mite younger, I'd go out there myself and beat those boys off with a stick."

Hank sat up straight. "That's exactly what I was planning to do," he said. "Thanks, Popper."

The old man apparently realized that there was no stopping Hank. "Now hold on. If you're bound and determined to go back there, you be careful, son. I know good and well you could take all three of them, Hank — in a fair fight in broad daylight. But it's gonna be dark and the three of them are lowdown varmints. Maybe you ought to bring some help with you."

"Good idea. Thanks, Popper," Hank said, as he headed down the sidewalk. But who? Clifford! Not that his friend would be of much use in a fight. But he had started all this gossip and it was high time he accepted some responsibility. Of course, when he met up with Clifford at the edge of town, he had to drag the skinny runt kicking and screaming back to the Cantrell farm.

"I just walked all the way back to town," the boy complained. "And now you expect me to stand up to the Leaches." He whined all the way back to Hank's house. "I'm not a fighter. I'm a ladies' man."

"If you don't come with me, I'll tell Mary Ethel and Rosie and everybody else in the county that you ran off on me the other night," Hank warned.

"Well, I already told them I chased off Lucifer and saved your life," Clifford answered.

"Is that so?"

"Yeah, and I also told them how you fell in the creek."

"And who do you think they're going to believe when I tell them the truth?" Hank asked.

For the rest of the evening, they hung out in the yard, tense as could be. Hank glanced at the pale moon, hung out in the sky as deeply blue as India ink. Crickets and cicadas fiddled away in the distance, blending their sounds with each other and with every other living creature out in the dark beyond their house. They heard an owl, then an old dog howling as if it were trying to swallow back its sorrow. A train called way off in the distance, as it traveled to those places of bright lights and swarms of people in the big cities.

The two young men waited until nearly midnight. Then, quiet as their own shadows moving on the ground against the light of the moon, they headed across the Greenfield Slab.

Slipping into the woods, they once again became trespassers, risking their lives.

Walking quiet as his own breath, Hank made his way through the woods like an Indian warrior camouflaged in the foliage, while Clifford cussed every rock and log he tripped over. Soon, they arrived at the pond and gazed out over the water. Bonnie's house was absolutely dark. Pulled halfway down, the shades gleamed in the light of the moon. Below the edges of the shades, the windows were so black, Hank felt as if he were staring into deep wells.

It was so quiet — too quiet. Except for Clifford and his persistent whimpering, not a single insect dared to let its sound rise into the night air. Then, silhouetted against the light of the moon, Hank spotted the ominous black forms of Orville, Junior, and Ferris, as they crept across the pasture in the direction of the house. Hunkering down in the weeds at the edge of the yard, the hulking shadows stooped to pick up a few small field stones and proceeded to heave them at the house.

They laughed as if they had been drinking hooch, their own homemade concoction, which they did just about every night. In fact, they were so drunk, Hank thought, that they could hardly hit the side of the house. Yet he figured he had better do something before they got lucky and broke a window, as they kept up their tipsy throws. They weren't missing for lack of trying. And knowing them, they might decide to pull out an old rusty gun and blast away at the house.

Winging one rock after another in the general direction of the house, they actually hit the gray clapboards twice, and once nearly shattered a window. Outraged, Hank snatched up a rock himself. It felt cool in the palm of his hand. He heaved it toward the guys — not right at them, but into the bushes near them.

"Hey, what was that?" Orville asked, the words seeming to run out of his nose.

Ferris and Junior hardly paid any attention to him. Hank let go with another rock.

"There something out there?" Junior asked with the same nasal twang. "Must be that ol' bull."

"Shut up," Ferris told him. "That ain't nothing but a rabbit or something."

"Maybe it's a possum," Orville said hopefully.

Hank considered bawling like the bull, but he doubted whether he would sound authentic enough, even with the three of them so drunk. After a moment, the Leach brothers resumed throwing rocks at the house, calling, "Come on out, ghost lady!"

Junior snorted, "This is just like Halloween!"

Finally, Hank's anger got the better of him. As clouds slid past the moon, his hands tightened into fists. Abruptly he stood up and yelled, "You get away from there! You go on home!"

They appeared startled to see him there. Then Junior said, "Oh, it ain't nobody but that ol' farm boy Hank Cantrell. And that half-pint Clifford Hopkins."

"You stay away from her!" Hank ordered, his senses over-taken by indignation as, fists clenched, he waded across the pasture toward them.

"You're nuts," Orville told him, his mouth hung open. "You think you two can lick the three of us? You ain't nothing but pups. And Clifford's the runt of the litter."

"Make that *one* of them," Ferris snorted, pointing across the pasture. Hank turned. Arms and legs whirling like the blades of a cock-eyed windmill, Clifford was sprinting away, making a beeline toward Hank's farm, seemingly with no regard for anything that got in his way — woods, creek, even the pond.

Full speed, Clifford ran right over the high bank and suddenly realized in mid-air that he was several feet over the water. He dropped like a rock. Amid sputtering and splashing, the boy yelled, "Save me, Hank! I'm drowning!"

Hank rushed to the edge of the pond as Clifford's head went

under for the second time — in all of three feet of water.

Hank scowled. "Try standing up."

Clifford did. As he stood up, he was completely covered with pond slime, duckweed, and mud.

The Leaches were overcome with hee-haws and belly laughs, but then they froze in their tracks, awestruck, like they were seeing stars.

In the doorway of the Hawkins house stood a pale figure in the light of the moon. Bonnie didn't say a word.

Finally she asked, "You boys looking for somebody?"

"No, ma'm," Orville said, gulping hard.

"If you're wanting to visit, why don't you come back during the daytime?" she suggested. "It's right late to be making such a racket. Otherwise I'll ask you just one thing — to leave me in peace."

"She's got a gun!" Ferris hollered.

Although Bonnie had told Hank she had a gun, he didn't see any such thing. He figured Ferris was just making up an excuse to run away into the night, which is exactly what the Leaches did, shouting, "Full moon tonight!"

"Ghost of Honeymoon Creek!"

"Watch out for the ol' spook!"

Orville hollered over his shoulder, "Old Man Crupp will be back here lickety-split with his shotgun! He'll blow you to kingdom come, old lady!"

Hank wanted to run after them, to stop them from calling her names, from threatening her, but he was standing face to face with Bonnie Hawkins.

The moonlight whitened the land, putting a bright edge on the hand pump, the porch, the chicken coop, the windmill creak-

ing overhead — anything that dared to stand up in the night, including Bonnie and Hank. From the absence of light in her eyes, he could see that she was deeply hurt. Hank wanted to apologize for the Leaches and for the entire universe, all in the same breath.

"Is that what people think of me?" she asked. "That I'm an ol' ghost?"

"No, Bonnie."

"Do they think I'm a spook just for being here?"

"No, Bonnie."

"And you didn't think I was a ghost just today?"

Hank stood silent.

A tear slipped down her cheek. "I thought I was kindly toward you, Hank. I don't hardly know you, but I had you pegged for a good boy. I never done you no harm, and this is how you pay me back? By bringing them here?"

He wanted to tell her it was just the opposite, that he wanted to help her, but couldn't get his mouth to shape the words.

"I thought you promised you wouldn't tell anyone about me being here. Now what am I gonna do? Lester and me got our anniversary in the morning."

Hank couldn't answer. After all, he had told Clifford which was equivalent to putting the information on the front page of the *Myrtleville Weekly Gazette*. And he had brought his jittery buddy here in the first place. Lamely, he said to her, "I didn't mean to. Really, Bonnie. I didn't."

"Then what are you doing out here so late of an evening?"

"I wasn't with them," Hank said. "I was trying to help you."

That was the wrong thing to say to a person of Bonnie's character. "You feel sorry for me?" she hollered, flapping her hands at

Hank. "Go on, boy! Get out of here. I don't need no kind of help. Just leave me be!"

Hank wished he could explain himself better, but Bonnie receded into the house, closing the door behind her.

She might not think she needed help, but as Hank walked slowly into the woods to head home, Clifford straggling after him, the Leach brothers' threat echoed through Hank's mind:

"Old Man Crupp will be back here lickety-split with his shotgun!"

Chapter X

As he glanced back at the pale light of the moon stretching across the silvery pasture, Hank told himself that he didn't know much about Bonnie, except that he liked her. Even though he'd just met her, he sensed that they had a great deal in common.

She loved the land as he did. He didn't want to see her treated badly, especially since she had next to nothing, and was asking so little.

He knew he had to stand up to Jake Crupp as no person, young or old, had ever done before. And somehow, he had to try to save his family's farm.

Yet as they walked through the woods, it was difficult for Hank to think straight — maybe because Clifford was making squishy sounds with every step he took and repeating, "I'm gonna die of pneumonia, I just know I am."

Suddenly, Clifford sprang up into the air. He screamed, "There's something in my jeans! It's eating me alive. It's a water moccasin. I just know it is!" He jumped around, yelling his head off, until a little bullhead flipped out of his pants leg, followed by a shiner and a couple of tiny minnows.

"You better hope you don't have a crawdad in your underwear," Hank remarked as he deposited the live fish back into the creek. "Or a snapping turtle."

"That's not funny," Clifford grumbled.

Hank remained prudently quiet.

When they got back to the Cantrell farm, Hank strode resolutely over to his pickup, swung into the cab, and told Clifford, "Get in." He started the engine and swung down the lane.

"What I need is a nice hot bath," Clifford said, slumping in the bench seat. "It's the only thing that'll save my life. Thanks for giving me a lift home."

"Later," Hank said.

"Later?" Clifford gasped. "Where are we going now?"

"To Old Man Crupp's."

Clifford groaned. "I sure as heck wish I'd never met you, Hank Cantrell. You're always getting me into trouble. You're bound and determined to get us killed. Don't you see I'm coming down with a bad case of the chills?"

"It's eighty degrees out," Hank responded soberly.

It was a warm June night, the air fragrant with wildflowers. The shoulder of the road was overgrown with the pink blossoms of meadow-rose. It seemed to Hank that most everything pretty was being squeezed off the land, until it hung onto the very edge, because it had nowhere safe to go.

He didn't know why he was getting so sentimental about the beauty of this place. But then he recalled Mr. Satterly saying likewise, "I been to the mountains and I been to the oceans, but there ain't a sight prettier than that patch of low ground, back of my house, when the mist settles in of an evening."

If a grown man could think and feel that way, Hank figured he could, too.

As they drove down the Greenfield Slab, Hank got more than anxious. What did he think he was doing? Was he really going to confront Old Man Crupp? They would have to roust him from his bed. Hank didn't know if this was a good idea. But he knew he had to stand up for Bonnie, as well as for all the other farmers in those parts, including his father and himself.

As for Clifford, his friend sat stock still, as if in a trance.

Without realizing it, Hank gripped the steering wheel even more tightly. The palms of his hands were sweating, and he kept swallowing as if he needed a drink of water, even though he wasn't near thirsty.

When they came to the long, winding lane that led to Old Man Crupp's home, he braked the pickup and read the two signs: *No Trespassing* and *Absolutely No Solicitors*. People said the man would shoot anyone who even dared to drive up that lane. But that was just talk. At least Hank hoped it was. It sure was dark up there.

He glanced at the trees that lined the lane, the tops blocking out any hint of moonlight. Steeling himself, he put the truck into gear and eased forward. The only sound out of Clifford was a soft, steady whimper.

On both sides the trees closed in on them. As they rounded the first bend, Hank lost sight of the road behind him. He felt like they were being caught in some kind of trap.

The lane twisted this way and that, and it seemed that he could easily lose his sense of direction among the trees. Finally, they came to an opening that turned out to be a sprawling lawn, behind which rose the immense brick house with so many dark windows.

In the traces of moonlight filtering through the trees, Hank observed that the property was well maintained, everything perfectly situated, almost strangely so. The house scarcely seemed lived in. In addition to the house, there was an immense white barn, seeming to glow in the last of the light, and a cluster of smaller white buildings — a chicken coop with windows facing south, the machine shed, silos, and corncribs.

"I'll wait in the truck," Clifford said, gripping onto the door handle for dear life, afraid that Hank was going to drag him from the pickup.

"Fair enough," Hank said. "I just need you to keep watch and tell Sheriff Rollins if anything happens to me. So don't go driving off on me."

"I won't, Hank. I swear I won't."

Hank raised one eyebrow in doubt, and sighed. Maybe this was a big mistake.

Cutting the headlights, Hank parked in the drive, got out of the pickup, and edged himself toward the house. There weren't any flowers to speak of, and the grass was trimmed perfectly. Nobody appeared to be about.

Hank eased up to the front door and was about to knock, when a faint noise drew him around to the side of the house, to the root cellar. He wasn't sure what it was he had heard, probably just a field mouse looking for a few kernels of corn.

Then, the lock on the root-cellar door jiggled ever so slightly. Somebody was trapped in there, he sensed immediately.

At the same time, out of the corner of his eye, he caught a glimpse of a huge shadow. Slowly, it grew and grew on the root-cellar door. He turned slowly to see Old Man Crupp, framed in a doorway of the barn, shotgun gripped in his thick hands.

It was as if the man had surfaced from the dark. He could have been a ghost himself. If Crupp had hollered at him, or said anything for that matter, Hank wouldn't have been so terrified. But the man only peered silently, deeply at Hank, as if pondering not whether to shoot him, but how to best dispose of the body after he had done the deed.

The blast that shocked Hank to his senses was not the explosion of the shotgun, but the roar of the engine of his truck. He glanced around in time to see Clifford gunning the pickup down the lane. Dust exploding from the back, the truck was quickly gone from sight.

"Gosh darn it to heck," Hank grumbled to himself.

Old Man Crupp grinned. "Friend of yours?"

"Sort of," Hank mumbled defiantly.

Old Man Crupp raised the shotgun and aimed it directly at Hank's heart.

Hank wasn't sure what to do, but he did know that nothing surprised a predator more than having its prey take a stand and hold its ground. So, fighting his own instincts, he stepped toward the man.

"Hold it right there," Old Man Crupp told him coolly, "You're as good as dead, boy."

Keeping his eyes level as he tried to ignore the threat, Hank said, "I want to talk to you."

Scowling, his fingers twitching on the trigger of the shotgun, Old Man Crupp asked, "In the middle of the night? I don't suppose it's about that batty old lady, is it?"

Hank recalled Bonnie saying that only weak people needed guns. He squinted at the man. "Yes, it is."

His seed-corn cap cutting a diagonal shadow across his face, Old Man Crupp said, "I know that old lady is holed up in that abandoned house. Orville Leach just called. He told me he and his brothers would've run her off if it weren't for your meddling. Said they wanted a reward, like I was paying a bounty on possum hides or something. I've got a mind to go back there this very moment, and bulldoze the shack with her in it."

"You don't need to do that," Hank said.

The man bellowed, "You're right! That old lady will be taken care of — soon as that lard bucket, Sheriff Rollins, gets here. Seems like he spends half his life in cafes all over the county. I been trying to track him down all day long. Fact is, you wouldn't be knowing nothing about her if you hadn't been trespassing on my land in the first place. Ain't that right?"

Again he had Hank. "Yes, sir."

They peered into each other's eyes, as different from each other as day from night. Finally, Old Man Crupp said, "She's just some old crazy lady. I tell you, boy, she may have lived there once, but that's ancient history now."

"She's hardly bothering anything," Hank countered. "She only wants to stay for a little while — just tomorrow. If you leave her be, I expect she'll be gone soon enough."

"She owes me rent then!" Old Man Crupp growled like he was chewing gravel.

"I don't figure she has much money," Hank said.

Old Man Crupp snorted. "What else is new? I tell you, boy, I've heard plenty of sob stories in my life. Her kind was all over the place in the Depression. Everyone was poor. Bonnie and Lester weren't anything special. I knew how to treat them."

He cackled with laughter. "Look at me. Rich as can be. And

Bonnie's squatting in a rundown shack that doesn't even belong to her anymore. But you wouldn't know anything about that, would you? How those sorry vagrants try to rob a man blind."

The heat was rising in Hank's face. "I didn't know Lester at all," he declared. "But Bonnie strikes me as honest and good-hearted."

"She's touched in the head, if you know what I mean."

"She is not!" Hank insisted.

"Listen, boy, I know a sight more about her than you do," Old Man Crupp went on. "The sheriff's already contacted the authorities. The best we can figure is that old lady must have up and walked out of some nursing home in Indianapolis. Lord knows how she got here, seventy miles away. But we're going to get her." The frown cut deeper into the man's face.

Hank had not completely understood what Bonnie had said about the heart of a man or woman being what mattered. Until now, as he stood facing Old Man Crupp.

Glaring at Hank, Old Man Crupp bellowed, "I know one thing you'd better believe! In an hour or so, this nonsense is going to be taken care of, good and permanent!"

"Permanent?" Hank asked.

"Since you're about to die, I'll tell you," Old Man Crupp mentioned, as calmly as though he was talking about the weather. "When that sheriff goes back there to arrest her, I'm going to blast her to kingdom come."

"You can't just kill her in cold blood."

"I can, if she attacks the sheriff and me, and knowing her, she will. She's got the motive. Just like I can say you came here to seek revenge on me for buying your daddy's farm. And I had to shoot you in self-defense."

Hank knew he had to distract the crazed old man, if only for a fraction of a second. "Just one question, Mr. Crupp," he said. "About your root cellar —"

Old Man Crupp went berserk. "You stay away from that root cellar!"

Hank made a break for it. Both barrels of the shotgun blasted directly at him, but Hank dropped to the ground. He saw the fire of the discharge and felt the pellets whistling overhead. Scrambling to his feet, he ran for his life across the yard.

As Old Man Crupp reloaded the shotgun, Hank plunged into the woods that lined the yard, just as two more blasts erupted. The pellets splattered through the leaves.

As he plunged deeper into the dense grove, Hank heard high-pitched laughter far behind him:

"I'll get you, too, boy."

Chapter XI

Old Man Crupp almost killed me. The thought rang in Hank's ears as he made his way back to his farm. He knew the man would hunt him down, because he had revealed to Hank that he intended to kill Bonnie. And he must also suspect that Hank knew about Angie Crupp. Were her bones hidden in the root cellar?

Soon as he got home, his hands trembling, Hank called the sheriff's office, but Gladys Higgins, who operated the switchboard on the night shift at the courthouse, told him the sheriff wasn't in. Which was typical of old Roly-Poly, since he was often "on patrol," usually checking out the pie of the day at the many cafes scattered across the region. Or else he was already on his way to the Hawkins Farm to collar Bonnie.

Hank's parents had gone over to the town of Sidell to visit Aunt Ruth, who was feeling poorly. The only thing Hank could figure out to do was to sneak back up to the old homestead, to see Bonnie one more time and convince her to leave on her own — before Old Man Crupp arrived with the sheriff.

Gladys happened to mention, "The sheriff did radio in to say that he was answering a complaint."

"Who made the complaint?" Hank asked.

Gladys said blandly, the gum snapping in her teeth, "I ain't supposed to tell nobody, being it's confidential, Hank. But I don't suppose it would hurt nothing. He's gone over to Jake Crupp's. I guess he's going after that old lady."

"Thanks!" Hank told her and abruptly hung up the telephone. Hurrying out of the house, not knowing what was he going to do, he sprinted across the Greenfield Slab and jumped over the barbed-wire fence. Straightaway, he headed toward Bonnie's house again. Maybe he could stop Sheriff Rollins and Old Man Crupp, he told himself, if he got there in time.

But just as he plunged deeply into the woods, surrounded by dark shadows and tall ferns, Hank heard a low snort. The brush just ahead of him shook violently. The next instant the cream-white bull Lucifer was poised before him — a gigantic package of hide, bones, and tensed muscles.

With a large ring through his nose, the ill-tempered bull slobbered and snorted and pawed the ground. Then he lowered his head and charged Hank.

Spotting a tree with low branches, Hank leaped to the first branch, just as Lucifer rammed his head square into the trunk, nearly shaking Hank loose like a ripe apple. He could hardly believe that Lucifer had him treed. How was he ever going to get to Bonnie? He could almost see her house from his perch, but couldn't do a thing to help her.

As Hank squatted on the branch, Lucifer became outraged, bellowing and shredding the bark of the tree with his horns. The longer he couldn't get at the young man, the angrier the white

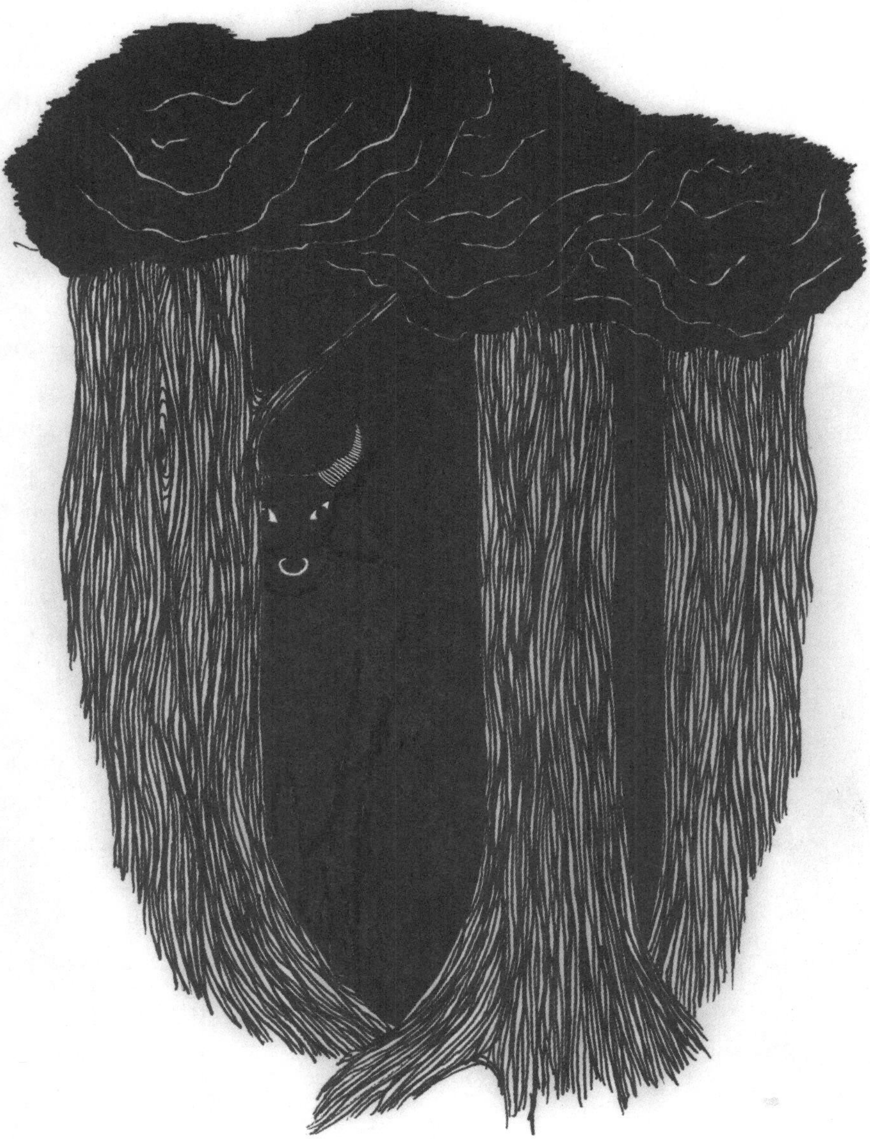

bull got, charging again and again. Hank knew he would be stranded all night, if not longer. Unless the whole tree was pounded to splinters, which seemed to be Lucifer's intent.

In desperation, an idea came to Hank. He stripped off his blue work shirt and shinnied back down the tree to the lowest branch. As Lucifer charged the tree, Hank floated the shirt over the bull's face.

The fabric was instantly pierced and caught fast on the horns, blinding Lucifer — at least for the moment. While the bull shook his head furiously to and fro, Hank jumped from the tree and sprinted down the path toward Bonnie's house.

By the time Lucifer had torn the shirt off his face and peered around suspiciously, Hank was well around several bends in the trail. He kept running as fast as he could, dodging dark limbs that reached out to grab him and leaping over tree roots that tried to catch at his feet.

Foiled again, the bull sniffed the air and snorted. Not ready to give up, the beast started to root around through the foliage, wondering what had become of the boy he had treed.

The sky overhead was a whirl of absolutely white clouds, sailing past the moon, as Hank bolted past the pond and across Bonnie's yard. He halted, instantly absorbed by the quiet. Not a soul was in sight.

She couldn't be gone, he told himself, not already. Yet once again, the old farm felt abandoned. The screendoor eased back and forth in soft rhythm with the night air, and the windmill creaked overhead. Conscious of his every footstep, Hank crept forward.

It occurred to him that no matter how strongly he held onto anything, it would slip away, because that was the nature of all things. Everything was elusive, just like the shadows that appeared when the moon was briefly overtaken by clouds. When he climbed the creaky steps to the porch, it seemed to be just the gray husk of an old deserted farmhouse. The black rectangles of the windows drew him forward.

There was no sign that Bonnie had ever been here. But he had seen her, he kept telling himself. He had spoken with her. She hadn't been a dream, or a ghost.

He raised his hand to knock on the door, but at the lightest touch it creaked the rest of the way open. "Bonnie?" he called softly into the gray interior.

The living room was exactly as he had glimpsed it through the window the previous night. Except now it lacked the warm yellow light of the kerosene lamp. The kitchen was empty, without appliances, only an old tin sink with a hand pump standing over it. The furniture in the dining room was layered with dust and cobwebs.

Upstairs, the bedrooms were sparely furnished with iron-framed beds. From room to room, Hank searched the old house, upstairs and down, frightened that he would come upon her dead body.

He returned outside into the deep purple of that June night, the darkness before the dawn — and found Bonnie fidgeting around in the front yard. Oddly, a crib quilt was folded into a triangle and tucked under her arm.

At his approach she started, as if he had caught her at something, and demanded, "Just what brings you here?"

Immediately, he said, "I want to apologize for what happened tonight with the Leaches."

"There's no need," she said. "You stood up for me, Hank.

And I should've seen that, but what with all the commotion, I kind of lost my head. I always appreciated it when Lester and my boys stood up for me. I got me a high regard for men who're faithful and true to their word."

As they walked back to the porch, Bonnie's gaze drifted around the old farm. "Why don't you visit with me awhile? I ain't got much time left."

Sitting down in the rocker, she carefully laid the pastel quilt in her lap, and Hank was certain that she was hiding something inside its folds. He joined her on the porch, but lacked the words to speak.

"What's ailing you, boy?" Bonnie asked. "You look as if you'd ate yourself a bushel of green apples."

"There's something I got to tell you, Bonnie. Old Man Crupp's coming here with the sheriff any second now. He's going to kill you, and me, too."

The old lady chewed on this news for a moment. "This very night? On me and Lester's anniversary?"

"Yes, ma'm."

"You know, it was seventy-five years ago tonight that me and Lester eloped. I was hoping to sit here with my memories for just a while. Well, when Crupp shows up, I sure as heck know what I'm going to do about it." Carefully, she unfolded the quilt in her lap. Lying there, ever so still, was a pistol.

Hank stared at the gun shining in the moonlight. "You can't do that, Bonnie," he blustered. "They'll put you in jail for the rest of your life!"

Calm as can be, she said, "I got a right to defend myself, don't I?"

"You can come with me," Hank said, his voice cracking on

the words. "You can hide out at our place."

"Bless your heart, son," she said, warmly smiling at him. "That's mighty kind of you. But no sir, I plan on staying put right here."

"You can at least hide in the woods, Bonnie, until Old Man Crupp and the sheriff are gone," he urged, getting more desperate by the second. "You know this land like the back of your hand. They'd never find you."

"No offense, Hank, but that ain't my style."

"You can't just shoot Old Man Crupp!" he cried. "And what about the sheriff?"

Bonnie said calmly, "You'd better hightail it on home, son. I don't want you getting mixed up in it."

"He's got a shotgun!" Hank said urgently. "I know for a fact he'll use it. He just tried to shoot me! He said he's going to kill you!"

"I'll be ready for him," Bonnie said evenly. "And if all goes right, he won't be bothering you or anyone else, not ever again."

As they were talking, the sheriff's black-and-white patrol car rumbled ominously across the pasture. The funnels of its headlights bent this way and that. Hank yearned to slip back into the night, but his feet were rooted to the ground.

As the car drew up alongside him, Old Man Crupp shouted from the window on the passenger side, "Hold it right there, boy!" Turning to Sheriff Rollins, he demanded, "We caught him redhanded! Shoot him, Rollins! Drop him in his tracks!"

Hank glanced to Bonnie, but she had vanished.

Sheriff Rollins, who never seemed to be in much of a hurry about anything, cut off the headlights and climbed out of the car. He strolled over to Hank, who met him in the moon-washed yard. Roly-Poly's holstered gun always tilted him slightly to the right, and the sheriff kept hiking up his pants because the weight of the weapon tended to pull them down. A squat man with a huge, round belly, his main recreation was chewing on unlit cigars, devouring at least four or five a day.

Hank hoped he was going to be jailed, which was certainly better than being shot dead. But for the moment, anxiously glancing over his shoulder, the sheriff only asked, "What do you know about this old lady, son?"

Deciding to act dumb, Hank said, "I heard she isn't real."

Sheriff Rollins squinted at him. "People say you claim to have seen her."

"Clifford and I went fishing here at the pond the other night," Hank blurted, his hands shaking. Old Man Crupp, who joined them in the yard, wasn't armed, as far as Hank could tell, but he couldn't be sure — Crupp might have a pistol tucked inside the bib of his bulging overalls.

"I know we shouldn't have been fishing here, but Clifford wanted to come real bad," Hank explained. "You know he's always looking for a little excitement. Well, when we were leaving, we saw a light. And I came back later to investigate. I thought I saw an old lady. But when I came back tonight, it doesn't look like anybody's been here at all. You see, I told Clifford, and —"

"Clifford Hopkins? That skinny kid?" Sheriff Rollins asked, cocking a sleepy eye at Hank.

"Yes, sir."

The sheriff turned to Old Man Crupp. "You hear that, Jake. You know yourself what a powerful imagination that Hopkins boy has, as well as a mouth stuck in overdrive. I figure he concocted this whole thing up out of nothing."

Old Man Crupp spat a glob of bubbly saliva into the night-blackened grass. "Not hardly."

"That seems to be the only answer that makes sense," the sheriff replied. It was widely rumored that he was afraid of the dark, and he did seem to be in a hurry to get out of there. He was more than ready to drop the matter, but Old Man Crupp insisted, "I know that old lady is around here somewhere! I can just feel it!"

Sheriff Rollins turned back to Hank and asked, "Supposin' the old lady is real, would you know where she is right now?"

Hank answered as honestly as he could. "Fact is, I was just looking for her myself. That's why I came back here, even though I know I shouldn't be here, since Mr. Crupp is awful touchy about people being on his land."

"The boy's lying!" Old Man Crupp roared. "She's probably inside this very minute. We'll find her. Don't you worry. You can arrest them both at the same time."

Holding onto his belt, to keep his gun from dragging his pants down, Sheriff Rollins agreed, "I suppose it wouldn't hurt to have us a look-see, 'long as we come all the way out here. But I tell you, Jake, I ain't seen the first crumb of evidence that anybody's been around here in decades."

"We'll check every nook and cranny of that house!" Old Man Crupp demanded. "That's why I pay taxes — for your salary!"

Sheriff Rollins suddenly got more interested in the investigation. "Okay, let's go," he said, hitching up his pants.

Chapter XII

Hank followed as Sheriff Rollins and Old Man Crupp searched through the house, upstairs and down, only to emerge onto the porch without finding a trace of Bonnie. "Where'd you get the idea that someone was living back here in the first place?" the sheriff asked.

Old Man Crupp sputtered, "Well, everybody says so. People've seen her!"

"Who besides good ol' Clifford?"

"Well, the Leaches called to say she was here," Old Man Crupp grumbled.

Sheriff Rollins grinned.

"Don't make me out to be a liar, Rollins!" Old Man Crupp roared.

"I'm not saying that, Jake," he said. "Only maybe them kids have played a little trick on you."

"You mean that boy!" Old Man Crupp yelled as Hank backed away from him. "And that little squirt, Clifford Hopkins!"

"Simmer down now, Jake," Sheriff Rollins advised. "Clifford

Hopkins could be at the bottom of this whole mess. You know as well as me that he's always stirring up the pot. Only thing I know for certain is that I can't find nobody living back here."

He clapped Old Man Crupp on the back. "What say we drop the matter? Let folks have themselves a little chuckle about it, and go on with our lives. Now, I could use me a little midnight snack. We could drive over to that all-night diner in Boggsville."

"Snack? You just finished a huge supper!" Old Man Crupp bellowed.

"That weren't supper," Sheriff Rollins answered. "That was part of an official stake-out. I was, uh, working on a case. Sort of."

"And what about this boy?" Old Man Crupp demanded. "I told you on the way over here, he threatened to kill me, then came at me. I had to shoot over his head to scare him off."

His eyelids sagging, Sheriff Rollins looked at Hank and said, "You been warned, son, that Jake Crupp don't want you on his land. Now I'll give you one last warning, and it's official. If I catch you trespassing again, I will lock you up, certain as I'm standing here. It'll be up to your dad to come and bail you out. And I know your dad, Hank. I don't think he'd like that a'tall."

Hank stared back at the sheriff. "Yes sir."

"Now be off with you," Sheriff Rollins said.

Hank turned toward the woods, relieved that they hadn't found Bonnie. Behind him, Old Man Crupp was bellowing, "But what about *my* rights, Rollins! Let this be a warning. From here on out, I'm taking matters into my own hands!"

Then, to Hank's dismay, the vague white form of Bonnie Hawkins appeared at the edge of the woods, just the other side of the pond.

The sheriff and Old Man Crupp stopped cold, as if they were looking at a ghost rising up out of the ground.

Old Man Crupp roared, "You see, Rollins! There's the old lady in the flesh!"

Sheriff Rollins appeared to be struck dumb.

Why couldn't she have remained hidden for just a few more minutes, Hank wondered, anxiously wiping his hands on his jeans.

"Remember me, Crupp?" Bonnie demanded, striding toward him in her long flowerprint dress and apron.

Showing his teeth, Old Man Crupp answered, "Yeah, I do. Not that I want to, particularly."

"You cheated Lester and me out of our farm," she reminded him. "You set it up so's that bank wouldn't loan us another penny, not even for seed, when our credit had always been good before. We didn't find out until later that you was in cahoots with them. Then you told us that you'd rescue us by buying up our land. Sure, we was poor, but we was never broke. Not like you made us out to be."

"Whether you like it or not, it's my land now," Old Man Crupp laughed. "And I want you off it!"

"Is that why you brung the sheriff?" she asked. "Because you're too much of a yellow-bellied skunk to do your own dirty work? Well, let's see you try and move me."

The color was rising in Old Man Crupp, all the way to the crown of his bald head. He yelled, "Why, you mouthy old woman. I'll take care of you right this very second. I'll strangle you with my bare hands!"

"So's you can keep me from talking about what happened to my poor sister Angie?" Bonnie asked.

As Crupp marched toward her, Bonnie slipped her hand inside her apron pocket and pulled out her gun. "You're a scoundrel and a brute," she said. "But you're not going to hurt me, not anymore, nor this here boy."

Old Man Crupp turned instantly to stone.

"Now hold on," Sheriff Rollins urged, backing away and raising his hands in front of himself, as if they could deflect a bullet. "Let's all simmer down now. We can talk this through peaceably."

"Peaceably?" Bonnie snorted. "That's all I asked for when I come here. I'll thank you to keep your gun where it is, Sheriff. This business don't have nothing to do with you, less'n you get in the way. It's between me and this pig-eyed excuse for a man."

Old Man Crupp had gone white, and he was trembling all over, especially his large jowls. "Bonnie, Bonnie," he begged. "Don't do nothing foolish now."

"You ready to die?" she said. "I know I am. I've lived more'n ninety-two years, and I'm ready. How about you, Crupp? You ready to meet your death head-on like a man?"

"Please, Bonnie!" Old Man Crupp sobbed. "You can stay here long as you want. You can even have your farm back. It don't matter nothing to me. Shoot, I only been using this ground for pasture."

"I know it don't matter to you," Bonnie said. "You let this farm go to ruin. Nothing ever does matter to folks like you, except to take advantage of people like Lester and me."

Hank was shocked by the presence of the gun gleaming in the moonlight and the transformation of Jake Crupp, the bully, into a tub of guts.

"I'll do anything," he blubbered.

Pointing the gun at him, she said, "For starters, you can apologize to Lester and me for cheating us out of our land. Then you can apologize to all the folks hereabouts whose misfortune you was so quick to profit from. And then you can apologize to my dear sister Angie for taking her life."

Even before she was finished speaking, Old Man Crupp dropped to his knees and nodded emphatically. "I'm sorry. I'm sorry. I'm sorry."

"If only I could believe you was sincere," Bonnie said, stepping forward and aiming the gun directly at his face.

"No!" Old Man Crupp shrieked.

Ever so slowly, Bonnie squeezed the trigger. Hank's heart beat wildly against his ribs. He was about to close his eyes, unable to look, when out of the gun squirted a stream of water directly into Old Man Crupp's face. Bonnie was toting a water pistol.

It took Hank and the sheriff a moment to recover. And they might have stood there longer had not Old Man Crupp jumped up and hollered, "Why you ornery old woman! I'll kill you!" Snatching up a tree branch lying on the ground, he charged Bonnie. "I'll splinter every one of your brittle old bones!"

Instinctively, Hank sprang in front of the deranged man. Although he was almost as tall as Old Man Crupp, the man was three times as wide as Hank, especially around the middle. However, Hank was ready to fight him.

"That's just like you, Crupp!" Bonnie taunted. "You always been good at picking on people long as they was small or old or weak! But I done proved once and for all time that you ain't nothing but a coward!"

Something seemed to give in Old Man Crupp. He lowered the club and gradually calmed down, and Sheriff Rollins told Bonnie, "Now that was some trick you played on us. But I think it went a little too far."

"I'd say I was merciful to him," Bonnie countered. "He deserves the electric chair, if not worse. Now, if it's all right with you, I'll be on my way."

"You're not going anywhere!" Old Man Crupp whimpered. "Rollins, arrest her, and the boy, too!"

"On what charges?" Sheriff Rollins asked. "For squirting you with a water pistol?"

"They're still trespassing!" Old Man Crupp hollered.

Sheriff Rollins pondered that. "It might be better to just keep quiet about this, Jake. After all, she sure did get the best of you with her little water squirter."

"The best of me?" Old Man Crupp sputtered. "Nobody's ever got the best of Jake Crupp!"

"Looks like somebody did this time," the sheriff said. "No offense, Jake, but you didn't exactly do yourself proud. Let's all just keep this under our hats. Okay?"

That's what you think, Hank said to himself. The moment he got out of there he was going to relate every detail of the incident to Clifford.

"Well, what are you going to do with them?" Old Man Crupp demanded.

"Evict them, like we planned all along." Turning to Bonnie and Hank, Sheriff Rollins asked, "Do you want a ride or are you going to walk out of here voluntarily?"

"We'll walk," Bonnie told him.

"See that you do," Sheriff Rollins said. "Pronto."

"I'll get even with you," Old Man Crupp said, glaring darkly at Hank.

Arguing between themselves, the two men were already walking back to the black-and-white patrol car. Bonnie turned to Hank and asked, "You coming or not?"

Hank trotted after her. As they continued across the moon-whitened pasture, he asked breathlessly, still shaking all over, "Where were you?"

"Those two was as easy to dodge as a couple of cowpies," she said. "I was hiding out in the raspberry patch. Lord, they're thick this year! I almost forgot what I came here to do. But I stood up to him, and all it took was a little clear creek water."

As they rounded the pond and approached the edge of the woods, Hank spied the white bull again — in the path directly ahead. Lucifer was on the run, at full speed, right toward them.

Hank shouted, "Hurry, Bonnie! You got to get up a tree."

"I'm not that spry," she answered.

Lucifer charged across the creek and through the brush. Bonnie and Hank slipped behind the trunk of a white oak tree, expecting the bull to zero in on them. But Lucifer kept on running — straight across the pasture at the police car.

When he saw what was about to happen, Sheriff Rollins managed to scramble inside the vehicle and slam the door. But Lucifer made a bulls'-eye target of Old Man Crupp's rear end.

His back turned, furious at being tricked, Old Man Crupp was still ranting and shaking his fist at Sheriff Rollins. When Lucifer's head met Old Man Crupp's ample behind, the impact sent the man flying sky high in an arc over the police car. Landing hard on the ground, he scrambled to his feet, only to have the bull chase him around and around the police car.

Safe inside, Sheriff Rollins watched the action. He decided to call Gladys on the radio to request back-up assistance.

And then, to his delight, he discovered a leftover ham sandwich in the glove compartment. While waiting for help, the sheriff munched contentedly on his little snack, as Crupp dodged and ran for his life around and around the police car — just inches ahead of the steaming mad bull.

Chapter XIII

As fast as they could, Bonnie and Hank walked through the woods. Old as she was, the woman still had strong legs, for which Hank was thankful. Bonnie said, "You're a good boy, Hank. I seen it the first time I laid eyes on you. I don't want you to fret about an old lady like me. You're young. Start thinking about that future you got in front of you."

Her green eyes sparkled. "I'm sure you got your eye on a sweet little girl. I don't know you all that well, but then again I feel like I been knowing you all my life. I raised five boys just about like you. Fact is, you're the spitting image of my Thomas. Now if you're smart, you'll take the memories and the good lessons we old folks give you and move on with your life. Everything dies someday. So, you got to live while you can."

"Why are you saying this to me?" Hank asked.

Bonnie's eyes went soft as she looked around herself. "Because I ain't never coming back here. I won't see you or my old farm, not ever again."

"Where will you go?"

She brightened. "I'm headed for Montana. One of my boys is living out there. I'm gonna take a last look at him and his wife. Then, I'd like to make a big loop around the country. You see, I got grandchildren and great-grandchildren all over this land. I'm gonna visit all of them."

"How will you get around?" he asked.

She peered deeply at Hank. "It's easier than flying — when you're gone." And she began to fade right before Hank's eyes.

"I'm sorry, Hank. I didn't mean to fool you," she said. "But if you'd've knowed I was really a ghost, my little trick on Crupp wouldn't have worked out right. You see, folks don't have nothing to fear from ghosts with squirt guns. It's only when they're alive that people have got to worry about each other."

Mightily short of breath, Hank asked, "You're not real?"

"I'm real as any ghost!" she cackled. "You see, I passed on a few days ago. It was only then that I found out the truth about Angie. I knew then I had to visit the ol' homestead and see that Crupp is taken care of."

As they drifted through the woods, she went on, "You'll say goodbye to old Popper for me, won't you?"

"We still call him Popper," Hank said, stunned to discover that Bonnie was a ghost after all.

"I bet you don't know how he come by that name," Bonnie remarked. "You see, he had him a Ford Model T that used to always backfire, so's you knew he was coming well ahead of him actually getting there. People'd say, 'Here comes old Popper,' and I guess it stuck over all these years."

She was fading quickly. Hank could see trees right through her.

"Yes, sir," she laughed, "Popper was a handsome dog in his

day. But as I recall, he didn't like to work much. He spent most of his time sitting around talking."

Hank smiled. "He still does."

"Well, send him my regards. You hear?"

"Bonnie," Hank asked. "How did Honeymoon Creek come by its name?"

She smiled broadly, tears in her eyes. "My Lester gave the creek its name — as a gift to me. You see, we never had money nor time for a honeymoon, so we had it here, right where we settled down to work and enjoy life on our farm. And the creek flowed on and on, clear and fresh all the days we lived here. Fresh and sweet. Just like our lives together."

Hank decided never to tell anyone, especially Clifford, that Bonnie really was a ghost. It would be a secret between the two of them, linking them just like Honeymoon Creek connected their two farms. They were neighbors who shared a common bond that would last forever.

Bonnie went on, "Those waters was once sweet as can be, but Crupp made them bitter with how he treated poor Angie. That's what made her ghost haunt these banks. And it's you who's going to set everything straight again."

"I'll try," Hank said, as they walked on for a while, although he wasn't yet sure what she expected of him. "You've helped me, Bonnie. A lot."

"Just how could an old lady like me help a strong young man like you?"

"Well, you've got a lot of pride in yourself. And you have a true love for the land. I wasn't sure about becoming a farmer or not — until I met you. It's what I've always wanted to be, but I just wasn't sure of myself."

"How can you grow up not loving it?" she responded. "You got this land flowing through you, Hank. When you put the dipper under the hand pump and drink down the cold water drawn from deep within the earth, you're imbibing its minerals. And most everything you eat — vegetables, fruit, or meat — is growed on your own farm, ain't it? You really are part of the earth. You're made up of the soil, Hank."

"I hardly know you, but it seems like my life's going to be kind of quiet without you," Hank said.

She winked at him. "Just make your own excitement, Hank. Don't wait for somebody else to do it for you. Rely on yourself. That's the key to it. And believe me," she added, "you're still in for a lot of excitement. Angie's spirit is trapped somewhere on this farm. You've got to find her — and free her."

"The root cellar," Hank said.

Bonnie nodded. "Could be. There's been foul play around here, and it all points to Crupp. All I know for certain is that it's you who's got to make it right for Angie. All I'm able to do is play a little trick on Crupp and nothing more. It's you who's got the serious work to do. You'll have to risk your life, but if you uncover Crupp's secret, you'll free my sister once and for all time — and save your father's farm."

"Crupp will kill me," Hank said.

"He'll try to kill you whether you go after him or not," Bonnie explained. "But if you can find hard evidence that Crupp did her in …. I wish I could help you, but this is a job for the living."

As they approached the edge of the woods, Bonnie slowly faded until Hank could see the flutter of leaves, a portion of the early morning sky, and the warm black earth through her very person.

"I've got to leave you now," she called. "You take care when you go after that black-hearted man."

Her body felt like the wind as he reached out to lightly touch her arm.

"'Bye, Bonnie," Hank called after her.

"Goodbye, son," she said. "And thank you. For giving an old lady the time of day."

"Gosh, that wasn't anything."

"It was to me," she said. "It was, and then some."

He watched as she drifted above the woods and pasture. As she rose into the sky, she was joined by an old man. Lester, Hank thought, as the man smiled and waved to him. Hand in hand, Bonnie and Lester floated over their beloved Honeymoon Creek and vanished into the soft light of dawn.

Briefly, Hank stood there, rooted to the ground, wondering just what was out there beyond his knowing.

Chapter XIV

Hank had to act quickly — Old Man Crupp might seek to hide or destroy whatever evidence was hidden in that root cellar. If Hank could prove that Angie had been killed and not run off, Old Man Crupp could be arrested and put behind bars where he couldn't harm Hank or anyone else.

Yet Hank suspected the man was just as likely setting a trap for him.

At home, Hank climbed into bed to try to get a few hours sleep, but the bright morning light — and the blur of memories from last night's wild course of events — kept him wide awake. Still, he tried to rest, knowing full well that his friend Clifford was snoring soundly off in his own bed. Well, Hank had a little something in store for Clifford.

Let him get his beauty sleep, Hank thought. Before he knew it, he too was snoring softly.

Towards the end of the morning, Hank drove into Myrtleville where he found Clifford loafing in front of Tremont's Drugstore and Fountain. The first thing out of the boy's mouth was, "I ain't said nothing to nobody. And I ain't going back to that old spook house, no two ways about it."

"I'm not either," Hank said firmly. "But I've got something that I do want you to tell everyone about." And he related the entire incident of the previous night — except for the fact that Bonnie was really a ghost.

"With a squirt gun?" Clifford asked, his jaw just about dropping to the sidewalk.

"And you have my permission to tell everyone in town," Hank explained.

Clifford licked his lips. "I'll get started right this very second!"

"Then we've got to go to Crupp's," Hank said.

Clifford gasped. "I don't think I heard you right."

"I'll explain later," Hank said, not wanting to delay another minute. He turned toward the cafe.

"Hey! Where do you think you're going?" Clifford asked.

"I've got to see Rosie."

"You sure this is a good time?" Clifford asked, suddenly anxious.

"I don't have any choice. We've got to be ready to act quickly, as soon as it gets dark! And I'll need everyone's help. Why don't you get Mary Ethel and meet me back here."

Clifford squirmed. "I'm not sure it's a good idea for you to be talking to Rosie."

Ignoring him, Hank strode down the street. Opening the screendoor with the Colonial Bread sign on it, he stepped inside the cafe and asked forthrightly, "Could we take a little walk, Rosie?"

"You want to take a walk with me?" she asked, startled.

He nodded. "Yes, I'd like to talk with you."

Luckily, there were hardly any customers. Rosie's mom told her, "Go ahead, babe. I'll keep an eye on things here."

Frowning at Hank, Rosie said, "Okay, Hank. But I sure as heck don't know why you'd want to talk to me."

She untied her apron and came around the counter. As they strolled down the sidewalk, Clifford tagged after them, keeping his distance.

Turning to Rosie, Hank said, "I've got to do something. It's really important and I wondered if you could help me, along with Mary Ethel and Clifford."

The cross look returned to Rosie's face. "It's so very nice of you to ask me all of a sudden," she said. "You know, we've been on summer vacation for practically three days and you've hardly said boo to me."

"I thought you didn't want to see me anymore," Hank said. "And I've got myself involved in a complicated situation."

Rosie raised her eyebrows. "So I've heard. What's her name?"

Hank said innocently, "She was real nice, Rosie. Fact is, she turned out to be downright wonderful."

"You don't have to go into the details," Rosie said frowning deeply. "I've already heard plenty about her from Clifford."

"From Clifford?"

"Yes!"

Hank sighed. "I should have known. Still, I wish you could have met her," he told Rosie. "You would have liked her."

"Are you crazy, Hank Cantrell?" Rosie demanded, halting flatfooted on the sidewalk.

Hank shrugged. "Well, I guess we don't have to talk about Bonnie if you don't want to."

Sticking her hands on her hips, Rosie asked furiously, "So that's her name? Bonnie?"

"Yes, but like I said, we don't have to talk about her right now. She's just this old lady I met."

"Old lady?" Rosie asked, peering up at Hank.

"Yes!" Hank said, perplexed. "What did you think?"

Suddenly Rosie appeared to be very embarrassed. "Clifford never told me anything about her being old. He just said you've been seeing another girl."

"No, I haven't!" Hank cried. "I've just been visiting with Bonnie. The old lady. She's ninety-two years old."

Hank threw a fierce look at Clifford who was already backing up down the street. "What else did that Bug tell you?" he asked.

"He said that you were crazy about this girl, and that you didn't like me anymore. He said that you were spending all your time with her."

"It's not true that I don't like you," Hank said. "Not by a mile! And he told me that you didn't like me anymore."

"Is that why you haven't been, you know, coming by the cafe?" Rosie asked. "Mom and I don't have anything but the cafe. Here I thought you'd found some cute farm girl with a rich father."

Hank cleared his throat. "I don't like anyone but you, Rosie, and I hope you like me. Even though I'm just a farmer — and I'm pretty much going to stay that way."

"Hank Cantrell, I could kick myself!"

"What for?"

"For ever listening to that Clifford Hopkins." She looked down at her white sneakers. "Truth is, I do like you, Hank. A lot!"

148

His heart soaring, Hank threw his arms around Rosie. "And I — well, I more than like you, Rosie. But instead of kicking yourself, maybe we should both give Clifford a swift kick."

Hank would have loved spending the rest of the summer making up with Rosie, but first he had to tell her, "There's something we've got to do this very night — and it'll be dangerous. I'm going to need your help."

Rosie frowned. "I would, but I already told Clifford that I'd go out with him tonight."

"Go out with him?" Hank asked furiously, glancing over to Clifford who was keeping away from the both of them. "I thought he liked Mary Ethel."

"Well, he's the only person who asked me to do anything this summer," Rosie said, "and I couldn't think up an excuse to say no."

"You can just tell him 'no' right now," Hank said, "Because ol' Clifford's going to help us — and then he's going to end up in the hospital. Clifford! Clifford?"

The boy had retreated farther down the street.

"C'mere!" Hank demanded.

Ever so cautiously, Clifford crept back to them. "Hey, Hank, how you doing? I see you and Rosie are having a nice little talk."

"We sure are," Hank said, grinding his teeth. "Fact is, I hear you told Rosie that I was seeing another girl."

Clifford tried to look as innocent as a lamb. "Did I say that?"

The heat rose in Hank. "Yes, you said that and a whole lot more that wasn't true."

"But you were seeing a girl," Clifford claimed. "You were spending day and night with her. Maybe I forgot to mention how old she was. It just kind of slipped my mind."

"And now you're going to pay for it. By the time I'm through pounding on you, you're gonna be as short as a tree stump."

"But we're best friends!" Clifford cried. "You can't beat up your best friend."

"We *used* to be best friends," Hank informed him.

"Don't say that, Hank," Clifford begged. "I'm sorry. I really am. You're the only friend I've got in the whole world. You're the only person who'll hang out with me, even though you don't like me."

"Why would you go and do something so terrible?" Rosie demanded.

Clifford hung his head. "I guess things just kind of got out of hand."

"I hope you've got a better explanation than that, Clifford Hopkins," Rosie demanded, sticking her hands on her hips and glaring at him.

"It's just that Hank's got everything," Clifford moaned. "He's tall and, well, you probably haven't noticed, but I'm kind of short. And he's strong, and I could maybe use a little beefing up. And all the girls like him."

"Like me?" Hank asked.

"Yeah, they go for the strong, silent types," he said gloomily, his lower lip sticking out an inch or so. "Not the little noisy ones."

"You're always telling me they all like you."

"They baby me," Clifford sulked. "They think I'm funny because I'm always talking, but never saying anything. I knew all along that Rosie liked you, and that I didn't stand a chance with her unless I did something. I'm sorry. I didn't mean for it to go this far. I'll do anything to make it up to you guys."

"Mary Ethel likes you," Rosie reminded him.

"But she's practically a foot taller'n me!" Clifford complained.

"Maybe you'd better realize when you're well off," Hank said.

"You're right, Hank, but can we at least still be pals?" Clifford asked. Hank glanced back at him, and something in his face must have been encouraging, because Clifford grinned and said, "Thanks, buddy." Hank didn't know why he put up with him, except that Clifford needed a lot of help and understanding.

"You can start making it up to Rosie and me by helping us," he told Clifford.

"What're we going to do?" the boy asked.

"Find a dead body," Hank answered.

Clifford's jaw dropped. "Say what?"

"I'll explain tonight," Hank said. "Just meet me here when the sun goes down. And bring Mary Ethel, too. I'll need her and you, Rosie."

"Why do you need both of us?"

"To keep Clifford from running off on me."

Chapter XV

Sandwiched in the cab of the pickup, the four of them drove through the darkness. Clifford was stiff as a board. "Maybe I should stay in Myrtleville," he suggested. "That way I can tell everybody where you are, in case you get killed."

But it was too late. They had come to Old Man Crupp's farm. Hank turned off the headlights and slowly drove up the lane.

As they neared the house, Hank told his three friends that he suspected that Angie Crupp's body was hidden in the root cellar. "I may need you to be able to testify that you've seen her bones — or whatever's left of her. All of you may need to be witnesses. Especially if something happens to me."

He still wasn't certain that he should be endangering his friends — Old Man Crupp could be anywhere, waiting in ambush. But if he got killed and there were no witnesses, Old Man Crupp would get away with murder again. When they got to the top of the drive, Hank pulled up behind a pine tree and cut the truck engine.

"I'll sneak over to the root cellar," he whispered, reaching into the glove compartment for a small pry bar. "When I break off the lock and open the door, I'll wave to you if the coast is clear. Chances are Angie's spirit will just fly off into the night. After all, she's been able to travel all around, especially along Honeymoon Creek. But I suspect that she can't really leave the farm until her remains are discovered.

"On the other hand, once the door's open, she might want to take her vengeance out on anyone close by — me or any of you. There's no point in all of us risking our lives just yet, unless you want to come along, Clifford."

Clifford swallowed. "No, it's a great plan, Hank. You'll do just fine without me."

"Maybe we should come with you," Rosie said to Hank.

"No, no. You go ahead, Hank," Clifford insisted. "I'll stay here and protect the girls."

Rosie glanced skyward. "What you mean is you need Mary Ethel and me to stay here so you won't be left all alone."

Clifford appeared too terrified to offer a protest, but Mary Ethel claimed in his defense, "Cliffie's not scared of anything."

"Just wait here and keep a lookout for Old Man Crupp," Hank said. "And whatever you do, don't let Clifford drive off on me again. We may need to make a quick getaway."

Climbing out of the pickup, Hank hunched down and crept across the yard.

The house was so utterly dark it seemed uninhabited. Hank figured Old Man Crupp could be lurking anywhere. As he scrambled across the yard, keeping low, Hank glanced around for the slightest motion in the silhouetted bushes.

Slipping around the side of the house to the earthen mound

of the root cellar, he pulled the small pry bar from his hip pocket. He wedged the flat tool under the screws that held the clasp hinge in place. He worked quietly, digging into the wood and prying the screws up, when suddenly he heard a distinct, soft "click, click" behind him.

Hank turned and there was Old Man Crupp squinting directly at him — down the twin barrels of his shotgun. "Now, I've got you," the man whispered ominously, the shotgun quivering violently in his hands. "Dead to rights."

"You can't just shoot me in cold blood," Hank said without conviction, because he knew that Old Man Crupp fully intended to send the blasts of both barrels into his warm body.

Old Man Crupp just grinned at him. "I figured you'd be foolish enough to come back here. Thought you could catch me at a crime, didn't you? But now I've got every right to shoot you in self-defense. After all, you're a burglar who attacked me with a pry bar."

Old Man Crupp spoke with a strange calm, his body shaking as he fought to restrain himself from shooting on impulse. "Of course, I killed Angie," he confessed. "I had to — she was going to leave me."

"You can kill me," Hank said. "But Bonnie knows, too."

"Nobody would believe that old lady, not without any proof. And besides, she's long gone."

"Don't shoot!" Rosie called suddenly from across the yard, startling both Hank and Old Man Crupp.

Peering into the dark yard, Old Man Crupp muttered, "What the —?"

Courageously, Rosie surfaced as a vague figure in the moonlight. She strode toward them. Hank beckoned to her, "Don't,

Rosie. Run for your life. He'll just shoot you, too!"

"But what about Mary Ethel and Clifford? He can't shoot them. They've seen and heard everything. They're witnesses, and Clifford can't wait to drive off for help and tell everybody about Mr. Crupp."

For once, Hank was thankful that Clifford was a dyed-in-the-wool coward who would seize the earliest opportunity to escape even a whiff of danger.

Rosie rambled on anxiously, "And the way Clifford talks, it'll be all over the county by daybreak."

"Where are they?" Old Man Crupp demanded.

"Over by the truck — out of range of your shotgun."

At first, his mouth hanging open, Old Man Crupp appeared stupefied. But then, overcoming his surprise at encountering Rosie and discovering that Mary Ethel and Clifford were off in the distance, he reasoned out loud, "'Long as I'm caught, I may as well shoot the two of you at least. And you're going to be the first to die, girl."

He swung the shotgun ominously toward Rosie. "You nosey kids should've known when to leave well enough alone."

Hank was too far away to lunge for the shotgun. He had to think fast, and he acted quickly in a last-ditch effort to save Rosie. Putting all his strength into a final, powerful pull on the pry bar, he wrenched off the padlock and flung open the root-cellar door.

Old Man Crupp swept the shotgun back toward him. "Why you — !"

At the blast of the shotgun, Hank was already swinging the thick plank door in front of himself as protection. Most of the pellets splintered harmlessly into the wood, but a few passed by the makeshift shield to graze his cheek and shoulder.

Raising the shotgun like a club, Old Man Crupp charged Hank — just as the ghost of Angie Crupp flew out of her earthen prison.

Old Man Crupp stopped dead in his tracks, horrified. He whispered in a weak, trembling tone of voice, "Angie! Don't leave me, Angie!"

The ghost floated toward Old Man Crupp, but she wouldn't offer a single word in response. She just slowly, silently, raised a ghastly finger and pointed in disdain at the trembling hulk of a man.

"Speak to me, Angie," the aging farmer begged.

Instead, Angie turned to Hank and spoke through silver tears, "It's true. My husband murdered me — 'his jewel,' as he often called me. But it wasn't simply because I was leaving him. You must know the whole truth. You see, I discovered his terrible secret. He killed his father — his own father. The man didn't die naturally in his sleep. His son smothered him with a pillow. And why?"

She jabbed her white finger at Crupp's chest. "Because he couldn't wait to inherit his father's land. And he wanted to buy the Hawkins farm and kick my poor sister and her husband out. Crupp's father saw the terrible greed and cruelty in his son's eyes. He didn't want his son to own any land, not even the family farm. He decided to disown the son who had disappointed him so greatly. He wrote Jake out of his will, and he put all the land in my name instead."

Angie floated over to face Crupp, eye to ghostly eye. "And so what did my 'loving' husband do with his 'precious jewel'? He locked me up in the cellar. And when I wouldn't sign the land deed over to him, he killed me, too. Now I disavow him and his hateful ways. You've witnessed my testimony. Now I can leave to find my peace, far away from this pitiful farm."

Old Man Crupp was so frightened of her that he couldn't look her in the eye. He buried his face in his hands.

The ghost drifted even closer toward him. Then, slowly, Angie's spirit began to rise, as she drifted up into the night sky to seek some other place, far away and unknown to them.

"Thank you, children," she said, briefly glancing down at Rosie and Hank. "I must leave you now, but you shall be rewarded for your good deed."

But when she had vanished, Old Man Crupp instantly recovered from his shock. He turned his rage back to Hank and Rosie who had rushed over to his side. "See what you've done now! If you'd just let things be ..."

His hands shaking, he shoved two more shells into the shotgun.

We'll never outrun him, Hank thought. He prepared to meet his death. His heart ached that Rosie would die alongside him. They would never get married and have their honeymoon, or settle down and have the children of which Bonnie had spoken. The creek would flow on, bittersweet, with the memories of their lost love.

At least Mary Ethel and Clifford would be able to get away, hopefully.

These thoughts flashed through him as he saw Old Man Crupp raise the shotgun — just as Clifford ran toward them.

"Clifford?" Hank gasped, not believing his eyes. But there was his skinny friend with a thin stick in his raised hand, headed straight toward Old Man Crupp, trembling like all get out, but with fire in his eyes — and Mary Ethel trailing behind him.

"You leave my friends alone!" Clifford hollered to Old Man Crupp. "Or I'll beat the living daylights out of you."

Old Man Crupp snorted. "With that twig?"

Nonetheless, the man appeared as surprised by Clifford's show of bravado as everyone else — especially Hank — but not nearly as much as when a commotion erupted in the barnyard. There was bellowing, banging, and then loud splintering sounds as Lucifer rammed through the wood-plank fence attached to the barn.

In a flash of white, the bull immediately charged Old Man Crupp. Before anyone could budge, Lucifer hit Crupp full-speed. As the youngsters watched in horror, the white bull trampled over the fallen body again and again.

When it was clear that Old Man Crupp lay still and lifeless, the enraged bull swerved away. Turning a circle, Lucifer eyed each of the young people — and fixed his horns on Clifford.

Dropping his flimsy stick, the skinny boy stumbled back-ward, only to trip and end up sitting on his backside in the grass. Head lowered, Lucifer bore down upon him.

Hank snatched up the shotgun that had tumbled from Old Man Crupp's hands and was about to shoot the bull when Luci-fer halted directly in front of Clifford. Cocking his head, the bull peered curiously at the quivering boy, bawled once, and then with his long pink tongue — licked Clifford's face, leaving a thick streak of foamy white slobber from the boy's chin up into his hair.

Then, as calm as can be, Lucifer jogged off into the night.

The four young people stood there, dumbfounded. Still in shock, Hank went into the house and called an ambulance. After that, he called for Sheriff Rollins whom Gladys located at the

Courtesy Cafe.

Old Man Crupp was still breathing when they loaded him into the ambulance. Sheriff Rollins kept scratching his head, not believing the young people, but there was the evidence in the root cellar — Angie's bones in the remains of a tattered calico dress.

There would be more questions, but they would wait until morning. For now, the young people just wanted to go home.

Hank was still on edge. He thanked Clifford, who'd washed his head under the handpump. His friend was so jittery that Hank asked Mary Ethel to drive Clifford home in the pickup. Then, turning to Rosie, he asked if she'd like to walk with him. Neither said a word as they strolled into the night. Then, still not saying anything, but sensing each other's energy, they broke into a run.

They raced, hand in hand, until their lungs were about to burst for air, until finally they were certain they were utterly alone in the thick woods.

Slowing to a walk, they made their way across the pasture. They passed by Bonnie's house, and Hank thought long and hard about his brief friendship with the old woman, as well as everything else that had happened to him over the past few days.

They continued into the woods by the pond, watching out for Lucifer. But they saw no sign of him. It was as if the old bull, like Crupp himself, had spent his rage. A fresh, tranquil atmosphere pervaded the woods.

Not saying a single word, Rosie and Hank just held each other's hands, as they walked through the night. When at last they came to Hank's house, Hank borrowed his dad's truck and drove Rosie home to her house in town.

Epilogue

The next morning, the bones of Angie Crupp were removed from the root cellar and later buried in her family's graveyard. To everyone's surprise, Old Man Crupp recovered from his injuries and within a few weeks, he went to trial. Head hung down, in a low voice, to the surprise of his lawyer and perhaps even to himself, he plead guilty to murder — of his father and his wife.

The next day when he was sentenced to life in prison, he seemed to be diminished in size. Curiously, he hadn't lost any of his bulk, but his arrogance and disdain had seeped away from him until there seemed to be nothing left of the man.

He erupted only once, and his complaint had little to do with the case. "Sheriff Rollins ought to be fired," he roared as he was sent away to prison. "The idiot didn't have sense enough to throw open the door of his squad car when that bull was chasing me, so I could jump inside. He just sat there eating a ham sandwich until I climbed on the roof of the car, and he finally wised up enough to drive out of the pasture."

To Hank, it seemed like the old man didn't even mind the fact that he would spend the rest of his life in prison. But Crupp couldn't stand the public knowledge of his crimes. He was furious at the widespread news of his humiliation at the hands of Bonnie Hawkins — and even more shaken by the loss of all his farmland upon the discovery of a written will.

The remarkable piece of paper was found in the cellar where Angie Crupp's ghost had been imprisoned, and it would prove to be only the first of two great surprises.

Not long after the trial, Hank and Rosie were sitting in the cafe leisurely sipping a couple of Cokes. They had drawn even closer. After all, she had saved Hank's life and he had helped to rescue her as well.

"Lots of people say you were crazy to get mixed up with that old lady," Rosie said, stirring the ice in her glass.

"But I had to," Hank said.

"I know," she said, looking deeply at him.

"How did you know?" he asked, grinning at her.

She smiled right back. "Just say I've had my eye on you since about third grade. I've been studying you a long time, Hank Cantrell, and you're not the kind to be doing things unless they're important."

People were still amazed at the news regarding the inheritance of Old Man Crupp's property. As the young couple left the cafe, they saw Clifford walking down the street, which wasn't unusual, except he was with his newfound friend.

"Wait up," Clifford called as he walked up, leading Lucifer on a halter rope.

"What are you doing with that animal in town?" Hank asked.

"He was left to me in the will," he reminded Hank.

"I know that," Hank said. "But you shouldn't bring Lucifer into town. He scares people."

"But he's like a baby now," Clifford said. "I'm keeping him as a pet. In fact, I'm giving him a new name. From now on, I'm calling him Cream Puff."

People were shocked to learn that Jake Crupp's farm had never been held in his own name — that his father had mistrusted his son so much that he had put the deed to the Crupp estate in Angie's name. However, no one was too surprised to hear that Jake Crupp had been so furious that he had killed his father in a rage. And that he then had imprisoned his wife in the root cellar and killed her, too.

But the sheriff and others were amazed to discover a scrawled document in the root cellar — a torn scrap of paper labeled "Angie Crupp's Last Will and Testament" — in which Angie Crupp left the entire estate to her sister, Bonnie.

Even more remarkable, when the old Hawkins farmhouse was searched for more clues, yet another will was found.

In that piece of paper, Bonnie Hawkins, "being of sound mind and body," bequeathed all of her possessions — which now included the vast Crupp landholdings — to be divided in equal shares to none other than Hank and Clifford.

All of the livestock went to Hank, except for Lucifer who was given to Clifford "in recognition of exceptional heroism in the face of extreme danger."

Hank suspected that some magic had been worked in producing this strange turn of events. But both wills were proved legal and binding. Old Man Crupp could do nothing about it except shake his fist and tear his hair in speechless rage as they dragged him out of the courthouse and off to jail.

In other words, Hank was now the proud owner of half of the huge Crupp estate, a good two thousand acres, including the old Hawkins farm. The only problem: as co-rescuer, Clifford had inherited the other two thousand acres. Hank would have the skinny runt as a neighbor — for the rest of his life.

"Isn't it great, Hank?" Clifford remarked, bright-eyed. "We're gonna live right next to each other. We can borrow tools from each other and help each other out with the farm work."

Hank knew full well who would be borrowing all the tools and forgetting to return them. And asking for lots of help.

"I thought you hated farming," Rosie reminded him.

"What do you mean? I've always loved farming and farmers. We're the salt of the earth," Clifford burst out. "Besides, I'm gonna raise exotic stuff like pineapples and ostriches. I'll be rich."

Maybe I'll move to the city after all, Hank thought. But still, he figured it was fair that Clifford was included in the reward. After all, Clifford had instigated the boys' first visit to the Hawkins farm. And he had finally shown some courage during the show-down with Old Man Crupp.

True to her word, Bonnie Hawkins never returned to her old home, but Hank was thankful to have briefly known her. Hank dreamed of restoring the old farmhouse and living there with Rosie, once they finished college and got married.

In the meantime, he and his father planned to work their home farm and the new land together, side by side. They soon were able to pay off the debt owed to the bank by renting out some of the land Hank had inherited from Angie and Bonnie.

On occasion, he and Rosie walked out together to the pond, just to gaze over the pasture. Hank and Clifford went back to being friends, especially when the squawk box did such a good job of spreading the news about Bonnie and the squirt gun. People were relieved to be rid of Old Man Crupp, and he never lived down his shame, even within the walls of the distant state prison.

Over time, the memory of Bonnie gradually faded, people claiming that she might not have been real after all. They said the Leach brothers were drunk that night and never had any sense anyway, and that Hank maybe had just imagined her. Hank did know that in the course of just three days, he had taken a large step toward shaping his future, thanks to the spirit of a very old woman.

As the years went by, the memory of Bonnie Hawkins faded in those parts. Only Hank recalled the truth, that she had been a ghost with a mission.

Hank certainly ended up with a good story of his own to someday tell to a bunch of kids on the liars' bench, for this was exactly how it happened. And, as the years went by, if he ever needed to be reminded that Bonnie Hawkins was real, he just had to look in his bottom drawer where he kept a photograph of her.

Only she didn't appear to be there. Where you'd expect to see the sweet old lady in faded clothes, there was only a patch of blue sky and the old farmyard in the background. But Hank knew that she had been standing right there when he snapped the picture, in the clear light of that warm June day.

To this very day, her spirit resides within the frame of that photograph, invisible, but still there, just a' smiling away.

The End